"ARE YOU AL[...]

"Sure." Longarm star[...] [...] saloon door burst ope[...] [...]d fire with a six-gun.

Longarm knocked June to the ground, rolling and clawing for his six-gun even as a bullet creased his shoulder. The logger was drunk, but he wasn't standing more than ten feet away. He missed again before Longarm could get his Colt leveled and pull the trigger.

"Ahh!" the man shouted, staggering backward, still firing even as Longarm's bullet produced a puff of dust from the front of his red, woolen jacket.

Longarm shot him once more and the logger crashed onto the boardwalk, heels drumming the wood. Whirling around, Longarm saw the first logger reach for a gun hidden under his coat. "Don't do it!"

But the fool was too drunk or crazy to listen. When his gun came up, Longarm shot him in the forehead. He threw up his hands and fell over backward.

"You!" Longarm shouted at the man trying to pull himself out of the watering trough. "Don't move!"

DON'T MISS THESE
ALL-ACTION WESTERN SERIES
FROM THE BERKLEY PUBLISHING GROUP

THE GUNSMITH by J. R. Roberts
Clint Adams was a legend among lawmen, outlaws, and ladies.
They called him . . . the Gunsmith.

LONGARM by Tabor Evans
The popular long-running series about U.S. Deputy Marshal
Long—his life, his loves, his fight for justice.

SLOCUM by Jake Logan
Today's longest-running action Western. John Slocum rides
a deadly trail of hot blood and cold steel.

BUSHWHACKERS by B. J. Lanagan
An action-packed series by the creators of Longarm! The
rousing adventures of the most brutal gang of cutthroats ever
assembled—Quantrill's Raiders.

DIAMONDBACK by Guy Brewer
Dex Yancey is Diamondback, a southern gentleman turned
con man when his brother cheats him out of the family fortune. Ladies love him. Gamblers hate him. But nobody pulls
one over on Dex . . .

WILDGUN by Jack Hanson
Will Barlow's continuing search for his daughter, kidnapped
by the Blackfeet Indians who slaughtered the rest of his family.

TABOR EVANS

LONGARM

AND THE GUNSHOT GANG

JOVE BOOKS, NEW YORK

This is a work of fiction. Names, characters, places and incidents are either the product of the author's imagination or are used fictitiously, and any resemblance to actual persons, living or dead, business establishments, events, or locales is entirely coincidental.

LONGARM AND THE GUNSHOT GANG

A Jove Book / published by arrangement with
the author

PRINTING HISTORY
Jove edition / September 2001

All rights reserved.
Copyright © 2001 by Penguin Putnam Inc.
This book, or parts thereof, may not be reproduced in any form
without permission.
For information address: The Berkley Publishing Group,
a division of Penguin Putnam Inc.,
375 Hudson Street, New York, New York 10014.

The Penguin Putnam Inc. World Wide Web site address is
www.penguinputnam.com

ISBN: 0-515-13158-X

A JOVE BOOK®
Jove Books are published by The Berkley Publishing Group,
a division of Penguin Putnam Inc.,
375 Hudson Street, New York, New York 10014.
JOVE and the "J" design
are trademarks belonging to Penguin Putnam Inc.

PRINTED IN THE UNITED STATES OF AMERICA

10 9 8 7 6 5 4 3 2 1

Chapter 1

United States Marshal Billy Vail jumped up from his desk at the federal building in Denver and smiled as he stuck out his hand. "Custis, I heard your last field investigation was pretty rough. How are you?"

"I'm fine," Custis Long told his boss. "Ready for a long overdue vacation, though."

"And you shall have one!" Billy exclaimed as his hand was engulfed in the viselike grip of his big deputy marshal. "Custis, there's not a man in this building who deserves a vacation more than yourself! I mean that. Now sit down and rest your feet. Would you like a cigar? These are fresh off the boat from Cuba."

Longarm accepted the cigar with rising apprehension, knowing from past experience that the minute Billy became too accommodating, something bad was afoot.

"Have a seat," Billy urged.

"If you don't mind, I'll stand."

"Whatever you say," Billy replied, taking a seat in his big office chair. "You've lost a bit of weight."

"It was a hard chase," Longarm told him. "I had to ride three hundred miles through some rough country to catch my man. And that's not to mention swimming two freezing rivers."

1

Billy shook his head as if commiserating. "Life out in the field does have its trials. You know, I was out there for . . . let's see. . . ."

"Six years," Custis said. "And you've told me about every case you had at least five times."

Billy's grin faded and he folded his soft hands on his desktop. "You don't have to be curt with me. I was just reminding you that I understand how difficult it is in the field. Our deputy marshals are overworked and underpaid."

"Thanks," Longarm said, slipping the Cuban into his shirt pocket to be enjoyed later. Right now, he wanted to keep his full attention on this conversation because he had a very strong feeling that it was about to turn unpleasant. "Since we're so underpaid and overworked, do you think you can get us a pay raise?"

"Ha!" Billy laughed, pushing back in his chair. "You know that I can't do that. Like you, I'm just a small fish in a big pond. However, if you keep up the good work, some day you just might land an easy desk job down the hall."

"A 'desk job' is the last thing I want," Longarm said without hesitation. "I couldn't stand the office politics."

"No," Billy said, "I'm sure that's true. But, if you want to succeed in life, you're going to have to learn how to be a little more diplomatic. How to be a good team player."

"Billy, can we cut the crap? You promised me two weeks' vacation the minute I returned and now you're giving me double-talk. Am I getting the vacation or not?"

"Of course you are. But . . . well, we do need you for one more important job first."

"That's what you always say," Longarm snapped. "I haven't had any time off for three damn years!"

"That's because you're our very best federal field officer."

2

"Don't flatter me, because it just makes me mad. What has come up this time?"

"We've got a pretty bad situation in a boomtown called Gunshot, in Arizona."

Longarm frowned. He'd spent plenty of time in the Arizona Territory but he'd never heard of Gunshot. "Where is it?"

"North Rim of the Grand Canyon."

"I've never been up there. Heard it is Mormon country."

"There are a lot of Mormon families settled in up there," Billy admitted. "But there are plenty of non-Mormons as well. There's also still a few wild bands of what John Wesley Powell calls the Kaibab Paiutes. I've been told it is an empty, arid country. One that is wild, beautiful, lawless, and hard."

"So what is going on in Gunshot that I have to go there before I take my vacation?"

Billy leaned forward. "We hear that Gunshot has been taken over by outlaws. That it's a haven for gangs that prey not only on the Mormon ranchers and farmers in southern Utah, but also on everyone else for a couple hundred miles. I've gotten reports even from the Navajo that the gangs coming out of Gunshot have been raiding and stealing on the reservation in the Four Corners area. These white raiders take cattle, horses, sheep, and women."

"Where is the law nearest to Gunshot?"

"There's a town marshal over in Cortez, and another in Grand Junction, but that's still a hundred miles or more away from Gunshot. We're getting reports that the Mormons of southern Utah are forming vigilante committees to try to fend off attacks from the North Rim country. Other than that . . . well, I don't know. Like I said, that part of the West is still untamed. There are no railroads or any real commerce up there that I know about."

"Just raiding outlaw bands, huh?"

3

"That's right," Billy said. "Brigham Young has been complaining for quite some time about the lawlessness coming out of Gunshot. He's threatening to form a small army of the vigilantes to go down there and settle the problem once and for all."

Longarm shook his head. "That would be a poor idea. I've never seen a Mormon who could stand up to a professional killer. They're generally hardworking farmers and ranchers more familiar with a plow than a gun."

"I agree," Billy said. "But if your back is up against the wall, and you're not getting help from the federal government . . . well, you know those people aren't going to put up with being preyed upon forever. And that doesn't even address the Navajo who are up in arms over their own losses. Two of them who tried to recapture their women were gunned down near a place called Lee's Ferry."

"I've been there. It's just a little Mormon ranch where they keep a ferry boat to take people back and forth across the Colorado River." Longarm scowled. "Billy, it sounds to me like our government ought to send in the United States Army."

"Possibly so, but do you remember what went wrong when they did that over in the southern New Mexico Territory?"

Longarm did remember. "It didn't work."

"That's right," Billy said. "The army went in there and, suddenly, all the rustlers, outlaws, and cutthroats vanished like smoke in the wind. The army stuck around a few months and there wasn't a hint of trouble. They left and the lawless element returned almost the following day. So the government spent a lot of money and got nothing accomplished."

"What do you expect me to do?"

"Go there posing as a fugitive from the law. A man with a bounty on his head. Infiltrate the gang and collect

4

the names of whoever we need to find, arrest, and prosecute."

"Aren't you forgetting a little matter of evidence?" Longarm asked. "What good is a list of names without evidence?"

"Good point," Billy admitted. "You'd need to ride with the outlaws of Gunshot so that you can later testify against them in a federal court. Especially the leaders."

"What happens if they decide to kill or injure innocent people while I'm riding with them?"

"Stop them, of course!"

"That's going to be a little tough to do if I'm supposed to be a man with murder in my past and a bounty on my head."

"I know," Billy agreed. "What we're asking is very difficult and dangerous. However, if any man in this agency can do it . . . you can."

Longarm thought about the challenge for a moment, then asked, "What about assigning me a partner?"

"Do you have someone in mind?"

"No," Longarm told him. "I prefer to work by myself, as you know, but this sounds like the kind of job where I'll need some help."

"It's a two-edged sword, Custis. While a partner would be a comfort and aid, he might also prove to be a liability. A partner would double your chances of being caught."

Longarm stood up and began to pace back and forth silently across Billy's plush office carpet. "What if the partner was a woman?" he asked suddenly. "A gal posing as a prostitute."

Billy's eyebrows shot up in question. "That would be a bit above the call of duty, don't you think?"

"She wouldn't have to practice her trade," Longarm said.

"Oh?" Billy half smiled. "And exactly what excuse would she use not to?"

Longarm frowned and considered the question. "Maybe . . . maybe she is reformed. Yeah, an evangelist. A female preacher bound to save the wicked."

"If she was a reformer, she wouldn't be going to a place like Gunshot."

"That's exactly the kind of place she *would* be going," Longarm argued.

"Those outlaws would eat her like candy. She'd be raped, humiliated, and run out of town if she refused to give them what they demanded."

"All right," Longarm said, "what if she is a missionary with the French disease?"

"I don't know," Billy said sounding dubious. "I think you'd be better with a man. A fellow outlaw. We can print up some posters on the both of you and it would probably work."

"Let me think about this for a day," Longarm mused aloud. "Perhaps the best thing would be to forget about a partner and go to Gunshot by myself. There is always the chance that I'll find some help."

"Yes," Billy agreed. "There is. In fact, when it comes to getting support, you seem to have remarkable good fortune in recruiting the help of women."

"Oh, bull," Longarm scoffed.

"Don't minimize your . . . uh, talents," Billy said with a sly grin. "You manage to get women to come to your assistance on a routine basis."

"Forget that," Longarm said, still pacing. "So what you're saying is that you want me to go to Gunshot and get the names of the ringleaders. Then what?"

"Get them to the officer in charge of Fort Cannon, which is located about a hundred miles north of the Grand Canyon. It's a small fort, but they're responsible for insuring law and order in the region."

"Then why haven't they put a stop to the trouble?"

"They've tried, but got the same results that the army got in New Mexico. They ride in and the outlaws either disappear or act like respectable, hardworking citizens."

"Do you know the name of the officer in charge at Fort Cannon?"

"I'm afraid not. But we'll have a letter sent so that he will be expecting your arrival in the next few weeks and be ready to extend any assistance you require."

"Tell the army brass and they'll tell the officers and the officers will tell the enlisted and then everyone will know that I'm coming." Longarm shook his head. "Billy, that would be a death sentence. I agree that I should pose as a wanted man, but I also demand that no one know I'm coming except yourself."

"There's no telegraph office anywhere near Gunshot. How would you even get in touch with us?"

"I have no idea," he admitted. "But I'll figure out something."

"This is a bad job," Billy said. "I've been wrestling with the decision whether or not to send you for the last three days."

"The next thing you're going to tell me is that you've lost a lot of sleep."

"As a matter of fact, I have," Billy said a bit defensively.

"You'll live," Longarm told the man.

"Custis, you could refuse this assignment. Since you're so overdue for time off, there wouldn't be any official repercussions."

"No, I suppose not," Longarm said. "But then who would you send in my place?"

"Walter Hamm."

Longarm scoffed out loud. "Oh for cripes sakes! Wally wouldn't last a day in Gunshot. He's brave, but not nearly bright enough to pull this one off. Save Wally for the simple jobs, like tracking down slow-witted cattle rustlers or bank robbers."

"I'm not going to tell Wally what you said about him," Billy said. "You know how much he likes and admires you. Custis, you shouldn't talk him down like that."

"And you shouldn't suggest sending him to his certain death," Longarm tersely replied. "I like Wally, but he needs to be in a desk job like you have before someone ventilates him with lead."

"You're out of sorts," Billy said. "And I can understand that, given what we've put you through the last couple of years. But I promise that, if you manage to get this Gunshot, Arizona, business taken care of once and for all, we'll not only give you that well-deserved vacation, but also a sizable pay raise."

Longarm headed for the door. "Tomorrow, when I come in for my travel money, I expect you to put the promised vacation and pay raise in writing."

"Aw, come on!" Billy cried, jumping to his feet. "You know I can't do that!"

Longarm stopped at the door. "You and I have been friends for what, six years?"

"More like eight, Custis."

"Okay, eight. All I have to say is the longer you sit behind a desk, the better you get at slinging bullshit."

"Custis!"

"Say hello to your wife and family."

"Would you like to come over tonight and have dinner? I think the missus is having a pork roast."

"I'll take a rain check on that one," Longarm told his friend. "Next time for sure."

Billy followed Longarm out the door and down to the staircase leading to the lobby of the federal building. "I'll put some thought to the idea of a female partner."

"Forget it," Longarm said. "It was a bad idea. I'll do this by myself the same as usual."

"Walter could play the role of an outlaw and your sidekick. We can have a couple of wanted posters made up for the both of you."

"No," Longarm snapped. "I like him too much to get him killed. Just leave well enough alone."

"At least you'll probably get to see the Grand Canyon!"

Billy shouted as Longarm descended the staircase. "I haven't had that pleasure in over ten years."

Longarm stopped at the bottom of the stairs, looked up and shouted, "Then why don't *you* take my place on this one!"

"Love to, but I'm needed here."

Longarm shook his head and crossed the lobby in long, purposeful strides. He figured he'd enjoy the evening and get an early night's rest. He'd catch the train down to Pueblo and then most likely buy a stagecoach ticket or perhaps even catch the Denver and Rio Grande Railroad over the Rockies into western Utah. From there, he'd figure a way to get down to southwest Arizona on his own. Either way, it was going to take a week or ten days just to reach the isolated North Rim country. Taking everything into consideration, Longarm reckoned that you couldn't hardly find a place more difficult to reach than Gunshot, Arizona. No wonder outlaws had chosen that as the perfect part of the West to raise hell and run wild.

Chapter 2

"Custis! Hold up a minute!"

He turned to see Julie Hancock running down the granite stairs, red hair flying in the breeze. Julie also worked in the federal building and had been chasing Longarm for two years, but he just wasn't interested, even if she did have a pretty face and a pleasing, effusive personality.

"What's the hurry, Julie?"

She took a couple of deep breaths. "I was about to ask you the same question. How come you didn't even stop by my office to say hello?"

"Because my hello would have really been a good-bye. Billy is sending me off tomorrow to Arizona."

Julie's jaw sagged. "I can't believe it! There are other deputy marshals here that do nothing but shuffle paperwork. Why doesn't Mr. Vail send them out once in a while?"

"There's a reason," Longarm said. "And it has to do with the fact that most of the men Billy could assign to this case wouldn't last a week in Gunshot."

Julie combed her mussed hair with her fingers. "Is that the name of the town where they're sending you this time?"

"Yes." Longarm shrugged. "I've never been there. It's along the north rim of the Grand Canyon."

Julie sighed, slapping her hand to her bosom. "I'd give *anything* in the world to see the Grand Canyon. Have you seen it before?"

"Yes."

"Is it as big and wondrous as described?"

Longarm smiled because Julie was a likable and even amusing young woman. Unfortunately, she talked too much about her personal trials and tribulations, making him feel edgy if he was around her more than a few hours. "Julie," he said, "the Grand Canyon defies description. It's everything you've ever heard and more. Maybe a mile deep and three miles wide, it is the grandest, most beautiful sight I've even seen."

"You're sure the lucky one," she said sounding depressed. "I've spent my whole life in Denver and I'd give anything to go to exciting and beautiful places like you."

"Someday you will travel, if that's really important."

"I'm off work now," she said. "Mind if I walk with you a little while? We never seem to have time to visit anymore."

"I know," Longarm said, feeling a trifle guilty because Julie talked so much he'd taken to avoiding her.

"Sometimes, I have this wild notion to quit my job here and just take off for parts unknown. Not tell anyone, but just go and see what adventures life holds out there in the world."

"Then do it while you're still young and adventuresome."

"But I'd get fired if I just up and vanished for a while."

"Yes, but they'd hire you right back if you wanted your job back," Longarm told her.

"Do you really think so?"

"Sure. You're pretty, smart, easy to be around and you work hard, don't you?"

"Oh yes," she said, expression turning serious. "I'm

12

never late for work and I always have the highest efficiency ratings in my department. You could ask Billy or any of my coworkers and they'd tell you that I don't fool around when I'm at my desk."

"Then there's little doubt in my mind you could quit, have an adventure, and then return . . . possibly even with a raise."

"Go on now!" she scoffed.

"I'm serious," Longarm told her. "It's happened before. Someone is sort of taken for granted on the job so they quit. Then the bosses quickly realize how valuable that person was and how unappreciated. So they seek the worker out, beg them to return, and offer them a raise."

"Wow!" Julie said. "I sure don't make much money. Of course, they pay the older women and men who have been in my department more . . . but I'm the most productive."

"Well, then," Longarm told her, "you really ought to consider taking that long-awaited adventure you've been dreaming about. Life is short and too many people spend their entire lives waiting for retirement or some event so that they can finally do what they've always wanted. I say that a person ought to reach out and grab opportunity by the throat and go with their dreams."

Julie closed her eyes and took a deep breath. "You really inspire me to do that. I mean, you *really* do!"

"Good," Longarm told her. "Now have the courage to act upon your dreams. Don't let anyone or anything stand in your way of happiness and adventure."

"I won't!" Julie vowed.

While talking, they had walked past the U.S. mint at Cherokee and Colfax streets and come to an intersection. "Well, Julie, I think this is where we part company."

"Can't I walk you home or something?" she asked. "You've gotten me so excited about opportunity and adventure that I just can't bear to go back to my little one room apartment and sit."

13

"Is that what you do in the evenings?"

"Not always," she said. "Sometimes I'll go to the library or the museum. Or take a walk along Cherry Creek and feed the ducks and birds. Or perhaps just do a little window-shopping."

"I see," he said, thinking that these activities sounded pretty dull.

"What do you do in the evenings . . . those rare evenings when you're in Denver?"

He shrugged. "I go out and have dinner and a few drinks. Maybe play a little billiards or cards. I might rent a buggy and drive out into the country or go see a lady."

"I'll bet you have ladies waiting for your call."

"Sometimes I do but sometimes not. Being as how I'm out of town so often, most women find other men to take your place during your absence. It doesn't bother me. I tell women right away that I'm the world's worst marriage material."

Julie slipped her arm through his arm and they continued across the intersection, just strolling along and enjoying the afternoon. "I don't think that is true at all. You're devilishly handsome and you have an aura about yourself that is mysterious and highly magnetic."

"I do?"

"Sure! All the girls in our office . . . even the older ones . . . they agree that you're by far the handsomest lawman in the building."

"Ah, come on!" he protested, secretly flattered.

"It's true. We've spent some time analyzing you and wondering what kind of a life you lead both in Denver and when you are out of town, chasing down dangerous outlaws."

"And what did you ladies decide?"

"We agreed that you would be a man who loved danger and attracted women of all shapes, sizes, and descriptions wherever you might roam."

"If that is true," he said, "and I'm not admitting that it

14

is . . . then I'd be the worst kind of man to marry."

"Yes and no. Yes in that you'd require a lot of attention, but no in that you are kind and considerate. You're a gentleman and that brings me to another hotly debated question among the ladies. Where were you born and where did you grow up?"

"West Virginia."

Julie beamed. "That's what I guessed! You're a Southern gentleman and you just have that hint of a Southern drawl that women find so attractive."

"Well, I—"

"Where do you live now?"

"In an apartment just up the street. Since I'm rarely home, it isn't much."

"I'd love to see it . . . if you don't mind."

Longarm considered the request. His apartment was a mess, with unwashed dishes and dirty clothes on the floor and on all the furniture dust deep enough to bear a fingertip message. He certainly didn't want Julie going back to the office and telling everyone that he lived in a pigsty. On the other hand, no girl had ever gone up to his apartment and escaped without having a tumble in his bed.

I wonder what she looks like without clothes? Pretty good, I'll bet.

"Are you sure you want to go up to my apartment? I've only just gotten back and the place is a mess."

"Then I'll help you clean it up," she told him. "I really don't have anything else to do and maybe we can talk more about seizing opportunity and the chance for adventure."

Longarm glanced away for a minute, thinking that Julie might just find more adventure than she bargained this very evening.

"Good," he said, squeezing her arm closer and quickening his step. "Let's go up and talk."

"And clean."

"Ah," he told her, "I pay someone to come in once in

15

a while and sort of sweep out the dead rats and. . . ."

Julie stopped in her tracks, expression stricken. "You're not serious! I can't stand rats!"

"I was kidding," he assured her as they continued on their way up the street.

When they opened his apartment door, Longarm stepped aside and allowed Julie to enter first. He would have liked to have seen her face but it was dim inside the apartment.

"Hold on and I'll push aside the curtains and get some light in here."

"It would also help if you opened the windows and gave this place a good airing."

"Sure," he said, doing both. He turned around and said, "What do you think?"

"I think you need a new cleaning lady," Julie told him. "This place is really in bad shape."

Concealing his irritation, Longarm scoffed. "I'm a bachelor. We don't spend much time fiddling around with decorations and the niceties. To me, this is just a place to sleep and change clothes. I spend very little time here."

"Yes, but . . . well, it's filthy."

Longarm hung his hat on a nail sticking out from the wall and then he removed his coat and tossed it over the back of an old horsehide chair. He surveyed his furnishings with what was now a jaundiced eye. Julie was right. The place was pretty sad. Maybe the next time he came back he would buy a carpet and some shades for the two lamps and some dishes that matched and—oh, hell, what for! He was not a man who coveted praise or sought to accumulate expensive furnishings.

"Do you have a broom and a dust pan?"

"There's probably one around here somewhere that the old cleaning lady uses."

"And some soap and—"

"Julie," he said, catching her arm. "I didn't bring you up here to tell me that my apartment looks like a rat's nest. I thought you wanted to talk and experience adventure."

"Well, I do."

He led her over to his bed then sat. "Now," he said, quietly, "you have to remember that it takes boldness and courage to be adventurous. To do things that you haven't done before."

"There are lots of things I haven't done before," she said, looking up into his eyes. "But I haven't exactly been shielded from the realities of the world."

He placed his hand on her thigh and eased her dress up a few inches. "Why don't you be a little more . . . specific. I don't want to make a mistake and ruin that image you have of me as being a perfect Southern gentleman."

"I never used the word 'perfect' because I'm sure you're not," she said, her voice carrying a slight tremor of excitement. "And god knows I'm far from perfect. I've committed my share of . . . indiscretions."

He pulled her dress a little higher. Almost to Julie's knees, still shrouded in a thick petticoat. "What kind of 'indiscretions' are we talking about?"

"Well, I have had brief but serious romances. Quite a number of them, actually."

"And how would you judge them?"

"Some better than others, but none ever lived up to my expectations."

Longarm pushed Julie back on the bed and leaned over her, his hand moving up under the young woman's petticoats. "And so you are still wondering if your expectations were realistic or not?"

"How on earth did you guess?" she asked, gulping hard as his fingers began to explore her most secret and personal places.

Longarm pushed Julie's dress up around her waist, then skillfully removed her petticoat and other lower undergarments until the tips of his fingers felt nothing but soft, yielding flesh.

"I would very much hate to disappoint you, Julie. But like I said before, you have to accept challenges in life." He sat up and unbuckled his gun belt, then kicked off his boots a moment before unbuttoning and shucking off his pants. "I honestly believe I am up to this challenge."

She stared at his huge, stiffening manhood, eyes wide with wonder. "I would say that you are definitely 'up' to the challenge. My, that is a work of art!"

He laughed, and when Julie spread her legs wide, Longarm inserted his finger in her slick honey pot to make sure that she was ready, then he mounted the eager young woman, easing his manhood into her with tantalizing slowness.

"Oh my heavens!" Julie breathed, "I feel like I'm being impaled by a horse!"

"A stud," Longarm corrected as his hips began to rotate in an easy elliptical pattern. "Tell me, Julie, did all your previous experiences end in an unsatisfying rush?"

Julie moaned and locked her long legs around his hips. "Yes," she breathed. "Always too rushed and too fast."

"And how long would you like this to last?"

"Forever," she whispered. "Please don't ever stop doing exactly what you are doing to me right now!"

Longarm hadn't had a woman in almost a week, and even though he could feel a hot fire already burning deep within his loins, urging him toward a fast and powerful release, he did not quicken or alter his thrusting motion, which he knew would give Julie maximum satisfaction and pleasure.

Time seemed to lose itself in their mutual pleasuring. Longarm could feel the young woman's heart pound and the rush of her fast breathing. Her lovely brown eyes were closed, but then would suddenly open to stare up at him slightly glazed and unfocused.

"I . . . never thought it could feel so good," she panted, head turning back and forth on his pillow.

He kissed Julie Hancock's cheek and gripped her surg-

18

ing hips with his powerful fingers. "Later," he promised, "I'm going to turn your breasts into pillars of fire . . . a fire so hot and gratifying you will beg me never to stop kissing and licking them."

"Do them now!" she begged, tearing at her dress and undergarments until her luscious, aching mounds lay bare before him. Longarm attacked them as a wolf might fall upon and ravage a helpless lamb.

Julie's shoulders rocked back and forth. Her long, slender fingers laced behind the back of his head, pulling his mouth harder against her until she thought that she might die of ecstasy. She would do so gladly, for nothing in this world could possibly feel so heavenly as this big, muscular, and inexhaustible man who was churning her like soft, rich butter.

"Custis, my darling," she half cried, half whimpered, "now I finally realize what it can be like when you are with someone who makes love like a Greek god!"

"You make me feel like one," he said, struggling not to quicken his deep, sensuous thrusting.

"Oh my goodness, it feels as if we have been doing this nearly forever. How long has it been?"

"I'm not concerned with time."

"Me neither," she gasped, "but I've never done it for more than five minutes with any man and I think we've long passed that."

"Yes, and we will go on and on until you beg for relief."

"I will never beg," she promised, pulling his face down hard onto one breast and locking her legs around him even more tightly.

Longarm didn't notice that the sun went down or that the streetlamps of Denver began to shine. He didn't see the first night star or the quarter moon creeping up over the city's irregular skyline. It was only when Julie began to whimper and plead that he lifted his mind from the perfect ocean of pleasure in which it swam.

19

"Enough?" he asked softly, kissing her eyelids and licking sweet beads of perspiration from her upper lip. "Is it finally time, dear Julie?"

Her entire body was shaking as if she had chills and fever. "My bones feel as if they have melted," she panted. "My heart beats so strongly that I fear it will explode, and the fire in my loins is ready to consume me," she breathed hot in his ear. "Please, please bring me to what I have dreamed before I die."

Longarm adjusted his angle of thrust so that his manhood would press harder and more urgently on that place inside of Julie where her liquid fire bubbled like molten lava. He felt her immediately rise and arch her back, ready to explode.

"Oh Custis, I think I *am* going to die! Take me now! Take me quickly!"

He took her how she asked with a few deep, perfectly executed thrusts, each as skillful as any ever used by a swordsman. And then Julie was screaming and bucking, her long legs waving wildly one moment and squeezing him powerfully the next. Each wave higher and stronger until they both collapsed, wondering how they had just accomplished something so perfect and complete.

"I can't move," she told him when she found her breath. "It feels as if my body has melted like hot candle wax."

"Don't move for a while," he told her, rolling aside and then lacing his fingers behind his head. "You don't have to do anything more than what you've just done."

"Custis?" she whispered, turning her face toward him. "Have I finally met the man that I've dreamed about all my life?"

"No," he said, perhaps too quickly. "But at least you now have a standard to judge other lovers, given your own passion."

She rolled toward him, one arm draped across his chest. "I don't think I will ever have a man like you again, so can I stay the night?"

"Of course. I'd be disappointed if you didn't."

"But I don't think I have the strength to clean your apartment and I don't think. . . ." she giggled.

"What's so funny?"

"I don't think that I want to spend whatever strength I have left sweeping and scrubbing. Isn't that shameful?"

"No. It's wonderful." He pulled her close and kissed her tenderly. "I'm going to take you out to eat."

"Must we leave this bed?" she cried, in mock protest.

"Only to eat and drink and recover. Then we'll come back and make love all through the night."

"I doubt that I can be as much woman as I was this first time."

"I'm not worried. You'll surprise yourself, Julie. And come morning, I'll leave you sleeping like a happy child."

A shadow of worry crossed her pretty face. "But, if you use me too much or too hard tonight, you could . . . hurt me."

"I'd never do that," he promised.

"I believe you, Custis. Are you taking the train tomorrow morning to Pueblo?"

"Yes."

"Then so am I."

"That's not possible."

"I have to go with you at least partway," she told him. "I know that you don't want me to go all the way to Gunshot . . . so I won't."

"I know nothing of the town except that it's not a place for a woman like you."

"And what kind of woman am I?"

He said nothing because he had no defining answer.

"I'll tell you one thing," Julie said, "I am a changed woman. I know that. And I know that I'm not afraid to go off with you. I'll see the Grand Canyon of the Colorado, too, before I return to my boring, respectable job with the government."

Longarm decided not to try and talk Julie out of this adventure. From what he'd seen and learned so far about her, she had never really attempted to do anything exciting, and now she was daring to give life a whirl. He would not discourage that and so he said, "We'll take the railroad all the way into Utah. I'll get a first-class sleeping car for us."

"Will the government pay for that kind of a luxury?"

"I have to go in tomorrow morning for my travel advance and Billy is going to raise a fuss about a separate sleeping compartment. But I'll refuse to ride second class this trip, arguing that I need to get rest that was due me on vacation. Billy will fume and bluster, but he'll get me that sleeping compartment so that we can travel alone and in real comfort."

"If he refuses to pay for a compartment, then I'll help you pay for one."

Longarm shook his head and grinned. "Dear woman, making love with you is all the repayment I need."

Tears filled her eyes. "I'm going to wait someplace safe in Arizona until you come back to me, and we'll ride each other all the way back to Denver."

"Where you'll be given back your federal office job."

"Are you so sure of that?"

"Yes. Billy Vail owes me too much to do otherwise. And there is always room for negotiation."

Julie sighed. "Custis, there's little doubt that everyone in that building will guess that we've become lovers."

"Does that bother you?"

"Of course not! It makes me feel smug, even proud."

"All right then, let's go get something to eat so that we'll have plenty of strength tonight."

He had to practically pull Julie to her feet because her legs were still weak and wobbly. She wrapped her arms around his neck and started kissing him passionately, so he decided without much effort that supper could wait another hour or two.

Chapter 3

Longarm felt as wrung out as a bar rag the next morning, when he went back to see Billy Vail. He collapsed in one of Billy's office chairs and asked, "Is my travel expense money ready?"

"No but I'll put the paperwork in right now and you can pick up the money before you leave." Billy leaned over his desk and studied Longarm's face. "For crying out loud, Custis! What happened to you last night!"

"I didn't get the sleep that I'd planned."

"You don't look as if you've gotten *any* sleep. There are dark circles under your eyes." Billy clucked his tongue with disapproval. "As one friend to another, I have to say that you need to start taking better care of yourself. You're blessed with size and obviously a strong constitution, but riotous living always leads to physical dissipation and early death or infirmity."

"Spare me the lecture, Billy. On my worst day I can do more than you can do on your best day."

"Now that—"

"Billy, you're thirty pounds overweight and soft as a stack of pancakes. So no lectures, all right?"

"You found a new woman again last night, didn't you," Billy said, unable to hide a tone of accusation.

"Yes, I did."

"Be more careful. Some women out there in those saloons have contracted—"

"This one works . . . or rather I should say, *did* work for you."

Billy's jaw dropped. "Who? Martha Appleton? I know she's been after you for years."

Longarm would not have told Billy if it hadn't been for the fact that Julie Hancock would expect . . . and need . . . her job back when they returned from Arizona. "I spent the night with Miss Julie Hancock."

"Oh my . . . no wonder you look so bad!" Billy cried, rocking back in his chair. "I haven't checked. Did she come in this morning?"

"No."

"Custis, that is a fine, decent young woman. I wish that you'd found someone I didn't know to dally with. Julie is the best worker in my department."

"She's taking a leave of absence and going with me to see the Grand Canyon in Arizona," he said without preamble. "I told her that you'd see that her job was still waiting when we return."

Billy's eyebrows shot up. "I can't make that promise! Tell her that I'll give her today off to recover from what was obviously a wild night of sexual debauchery. But I fully expect to see her at her desk in the morning."

"She craves excitement," Longarm said. "The kid needs a break and that's why I'm letting her come part of the way to Gunshot with me."

Billy wasn't pleased. He scowled and then clenched one of his soft, small fists and pounded his desk. "I like Miss Hancock very much and I fully disapprove of this relationship. Nothing good or lasting will come of it and you'll leave her with a broken heart."

"Julie wasn't a virgin and I didn't seduce her," Longarm snapped, feeling offended. "It wasn't even my idea that she leave work for a few weeks and come away with

24

me to Arizona. It was her idea all the way, but I'm glad she is temporarily kicking off the traces and going west for some long overdue adventure."

"If she goes to Gunshot, she'll get a whole lot more than 'adventure,' " Billy warned.

"She won't go to Gunshot. I'll make sure of that. But I must have enough travel money so that we can go first class with a private sleeping compartment."

Billy laughed outright, then cried, "Custis, do you really believe that the government is going to subsidize your little dalliance?"

"My what?"

"Your tryst. Your sordid affair. Absolutely not!"

"Then I'll refuse this miserable assignment," Longarm told his boss, while rising from his seat. "And I'll take Julie west on my own dime for a taste of adventure and my long overdue vacation."

"You wouldn't!"

"Test me," Longarm challenged. "I don't ask much and I do more than any other three of your deputy marshals. So this is what I want and how it will be or we're both going on vacation."

Billy opened his mouth to shout or protest, then seemed to realize that it would be pointless. That he had no choice but to give in to this demand and offer both his best office worker and deputy marshal his well wishes.

"You have me over a barrel," he said peevishly. "I'll put in for a couple of first-class accommodations. We've also made up four wanted posters on you using a sketch that I think flatters your ugly mug."

"How much is the reward on my head?"

"Five hundred dollars."

"I'm worth more," Longarm said. "What is it that I'm supposed to have done?"

"The last one we used on you we said you were wanted for bank robbery in Texas. We changed this one to say that you gunned down a marshal in Laramie, Wyoming."

Longarm shook his head. "Seems like that ought to be worth more than five hundred."

"The fella you shot wasn't much of a marshal."

"I'll pick up the wanted posters and the travel money. Thanks for finally sending me on something better than a mule train. First class with Julie is going to be special."

"Yeah, well, all I have to say is that you'd better return from Gunshot with positive results . . . as well as my best office worker."

"I will."

"If you don't slow down with Miss Hancock, there probably won't be anything left of either of you by the time you disembark in Arizona."

"You're just jealous."

Billy barked a hollow laugh, shrugged his shoulders, and managed a smile. "Actually, you're right. I'm a happily married man and I'd never cheat on my dear wife but . . . well, a fella can't help but wonder what it would be like to spend the night with someone like Miss Hancock."

"Take your wildest fantasy and multiply it by ten," Longarm said feeling a bit irascible. "And that's what it's like to make love to Julie."

Billy sighed. "You didn't need to say that."

"No," Longarm said as he left, "but it's the simple truth."

The next few hours went by quickly, and when the train pulled out of Denver heading south, Longarm escorted Julie down the aisle of the first-class coach until he came to the porter.

"Hello, Marshal Long," the porter said. "Seems like you were with us just a few weeks ago."

"I was. Had some trouble down in Santa Fe."

"Well, I'm afraid," the porter stammered, unable to keep his eyes off Julie, "you're in the wrong coach. Third class is five cars to the rear."

"We're traveling *first-class* this trip," Longarm told the porter. "We've got a private compartment. Number seven."

The man inspected his tickets carefully. "We'll I'll be! You must have done something awfully important to get this kind of treatment from the government."

"I did do something important. I brought this young lady along."

The porter blushed and so did Julie, but nothing more was said until they reached the compartment. "It's small," the porter apologized. "Upper and lower bunks and a little fold out table. But . . ."

"We'll do just fine," Longarm replied, slipping the man a fifty-cent piece and easing Julie inside. "What time is dinner in the dining car?"

"Six o'clock."

"We'll be there," Longarm promised, closing the door behind them.

"It's cozy," Julie said, flushed with excitement.

Longarm agreed. Besides the bunks, there were two small but nicely upholstered seats facing each other. Their window was large, and it had recently been cleaned.

"I think I'm going to really enjoy this trip," Longarm said, taking Julie into his arms and kissing her.

She began kissing him back and soon they were pulling off each other's clothing and then Longarm sat down on the seat and Julie straddled him.

"This is heavenly," she breathed.

"Yes, it is," he agreed. "We don't even have to move."

She leaned back and studied his face. "What do you mean?"

As if on cue, the train jolted forward, driving Longarm's rod deeper into Julie, who squealed with surprise and pleasure. "Oh goodness, that was quite a start!"

"Pretty soon we'll get up some speed and this coach will start bumping and rocking like cork on a creek. You're going to love how it feels."

27

"I can hardly wait." Julie wiggled her bottom and rested her head on his shoulder, gazing out the window. They were high enough so that there was no reason to worry about anyone seeing them making love.

True to his promise, as the train picked up speed, its movement became more pronounced. Julie began to breathe harder and squirm with pleasure. "This is wonderful!"

"It only gets better," he promised.

Julie gripped his shoulders and positioned herself for maximum pleasure. Soon she was biting her lower lip trying not to scream because it felt so good.

"How long will it take us this time?" she asked.

"We should probably finish before reaching Colorado Springs," Longarm replied with a straight face as his own pleasure increased. "Just hold tight and don't worry about crying out. The train is noisy enough that we can holler and shout."

"I love this journey already," she told him as her fingernails bit into the lapels of his jacket and her slim but muscular buttocks began to contract with regularity.

The trip down to Pueblo was far too brief, but they had managed to eat well, make love most of their waking hours, and sleep soundly when they tumbled into their individual bunks. Longarm wished that they were traveling around the world.

In Pueblo, they boarded the Denver and Rio Grande, a much more utilitarian railroad. Longarm tried to get them a private compartment, but they were all occupied.

"How sad!" Julie whispered as they were forced to settle for a hard, wooden bench in the third-class coach, where rough men and women stared at them suspiciously. "We're spoiled."

"It will get worse when we are forced to travel across southeastern Utah. We'll either buy horses or tickets on a stagecoach, which will make even this poor arrangement seem elegant and comfortable."

"How disappointing," she said, holding his hand and leaning her head onto his chest so that she could rest.

For the next three days, Longarm and Julie traveled over the Rocky Mountains. At night, their train would pull into a small logging or mining town and the passengers would either stay on board or find a hotel room. Longarm preferred the latter. He had often traveled this route and knew where the best hotels were to be found as well as the favorite cafes. High in the Rockies, the towns were rough but picturesque, and they reveled in the scent of pines.

"I love it up here," Julie told him one evening as they strolled hand in hand down the dusty main street of a little town called Silver Creek. "I could live in a small logging community like this. Could you?"

Longarm shook his head. "I like Denver. There's more to do and see. I'd get cabin fever up here and the winters would be twice as bad as we have in the city."

"Hmmm," Julie mused. "I might not like that so much. Probably have snow up to the rafters, huh?"

"At least. We're probably about twelve thousand feet elevation. The first snows will start falling early in October and this place will be buried until late in March."

"That may be true," she said, "but it is perfect right now."

Longarm was about to agree when three burly loggers crashed out of a saloon and slammed into Julie, knocking her to the ground.

"Hey!" one of them said, gazing down at her with hungry, bloodshot eyes. "You're kinda pretty. What's your name?"

The lumberjack had a thick, black beard. Longarm grabbed it. "You owe her an apology, mister."

The big man's eyes widened and his breath reeked of

29

whiskey. "By gawd, you're right. I'll just help the little woman up right now."

He looked at his two equally drunk and grinning friends, then bent over and grabbed Julie under the arms and set her on her feet. "I sure am sorry, miss."

"That's all right," she said, slapping dirt from her dress.

"Glad to hear you say that," the lumberjack said, snatching off his cap to reveal a second bush of wild, unruly hair. "Now how about a little kiss just so I know that there's no hard feelings?"

"Get out of here," Longarm growled, giving the man a hard shove that sent him sprawling into the street.

"Dammit," one of his companions protested. "You can't do that to Olaf!"

"I just did. Now move along and behave yourselves."

"Who the hell you think you are!" the second man shouted, throwing a punch at Longarm's head.

He easily ducked the punch and delivered a crunching uppercut to the man's jaw, sending him flying back into the saloon. The third lumberjack roared and tackled Longarm, driving him off the boardwalk and into the street.

Then both the first and the third man pounced on him and it was all that Longarm could do to roll out from under the weight of their bodies. He jumped to his feet, kicked one in the crotch, then punched the other man in the nose with a left jab and followed it with a right cross that sent him backpedaling into a horse trough.

"All you all right?" Julie asked, rushing into the street to stand at his side.

"Sure." Longarm started to say something else when the saloon door burst open and the remaining logger opened fire with a six-gun.

Longarm knocked Julie to the ground, and rolled and clawed for his own six-gun even as a bullet creased his shoulder. The logger was drunk, but he wasn't standing more then ten feet away. He missed again before Longarm could get his Colt leveled and pull the trigger.

"Ahh!" the man shouted, staggering backward, still firing even as Longarm's bullet produced a puff of dust from the front of his red, woolen jacket.

Longarm shot him once more and the logger crashed onto the boardwalk, heels drumming the wood. Whirling around, Longarm saw the first logger reach for a gun hidden under his coat. "Don't do it!"

But the fool was too drunk or crazy to listen. When his gun came up, Longarm shot him in the forehead. He threw up his hands and fell over backward.

"You!" Longarm shouted at the man trying to pull himself out of the watering trough. "Don't move."

"Go to hell!" the logger cried, rolling to the ground and fumbling in his pocket for a weapon.

Longarm saw the Bowie knife and knew that he ought to kill the last of this trio. It was one thing to get drunk and rowdy, another thing to pull a gun or a knife with the intent to kill.

"Freeze!" Longarm ordered.

The logger charged forward with a knife in his hand. Longarm raised his Colt and shot at the onrushing lumberjack a few more times, but the man kept coming.

Longarm knew his gun was empty. He jumped forward, grabbed the logger's wrist, and slammed it against a porch post three times before the knife spun away. The logger tried to bite Longarm's face but he stomped down onto the dying man's foot and then tripped him to the ground.

"Stay down!" he shouted.

The man struggled to rise with a bloody froth on his lips. "You . . . you sonofabitch!" he gasped a moment before he toppled forward in death.

Longarm rushed over to Julie. "Are you all right?"

"Yes, but did you really have to kill all of them?"

"What else was I going to do?"

"Couldn't you have pistol whipped them or something?"

"I might have," he told her, "if I'd been alone. But what

if that turned out to be a mistake? Then what might have happened to you?"

She hugged him tight as men poured out of the saloons to see the carnage. "Custis," she whispered, "can we go back to our hotel room now?"

"Sure," he said, turning to look at the gawkers and shouting so that everyone could hear his voice. "Those three men knocked down this lady then tried to kill me. I'm a United States deputy marshal and I won't tolerate lawlessness. Someone get those bodies off the street and buried."

"Who'll pay for them?" a lumberjack asked, folding his arms across his chest and sticking out his jaw. "They were working men, but they spent all their earnings on whiskey and cards."

"Then take up a collection," Longarm replied.

The loggers were mad. Three of their friends had just died in a hail of gunfire, and now they were being asked to pay for their burial.

Longarm heard the rumblings, but he knew that the trio would get planted come morning. And by then, he and Julie would be on their way to Gunshot, Arizona.

Chapter 4

For the next week, Longarm and Julia traveled by train, then by coach, and finally they bought a couple of good saddle horses from a horse trader they met just outside of Four Corners.

"This little fella is a perfect size for the lady," the trader confidently told them. "Gentle and a bit long in the tooth, but he's still got a lot of miles left in him."

"What's his history?" Longarm asked.

"I bought him from some Navajo kids a week or two ago. There were three of them riding him all at once."

"He's old as dirt and ugly," Longarm said, noting the animal's jug head.

"No he isn't!" Julie cried. "I love him! He's just the right size."

"How much?" Longarm wanted to know.

"Fifty dollars."

"He's worth ten and I'll give you twenty providing you throw in that old Indian saddle."

"Not a chance," the dirty and nervous-looking horse trader said, wagging his chin back and forth. "But I might be talked into taking forty dollars."

"Thirty and that's my offer."

"Okay," the man agreed, sounding like he'd just sold his mother. "What about a horse for you?"

The horse trader had a string of seven, and Longarm picked out a big buckskin with straight legs and a deep chest. "I'm going to ride him first."

"Of course," the trader said. "I aim to please. I've never sold anybody a bad horse in my entire life."

Longarm had the trader saddle the buckskin. He rode the tall horse at a walk, trot, and gallop. The animal reined well, possessed smooth gaits, and had a soft mouth. He would back up, and when Longarm picked up the hooves, he could see that the buckskin had good, hard, black hooves not prone to cracks or chipping.

"He's an exceptional animal, ain't he?" the horse trader said. "Mister, you got a real eye for good horseflesh."

"How much do you want for him?"

"A hundred for the horse and the saddle you're sitting in."

"Seventy," Longarm grunted.

"Eighty-five and you also get the bridle, bit, horse blanket, and a lead rope."

"I'll go up to eighty if you throw in two pair of hobbles along with one of those sacks of oats I see tied to your pack mule."

"It's a deal," the horse trader said, again acting like he'd gotten skinned. "So let's see now, you owe me one hundred ten dollars for the buckskin, the Navajo pony, two saddles, bridles, blankets, and a sack of oats."

"That's right."

"Mister, you sure do drive a hard bargain. Why, if I had to deal with the likes of you every day, then I'd go broke."

"You'll go broke when hell freezes over," Longarm said dryly as he found his money.

"Well, sir," the horse trader said when Longarm had counted out the cash, "it sure has been a pleasure doing business with you. Stranger, what's your name?"

34

"United States Deputy Marshal Custis Long."

The horse trader's jaw dropped and he gulped. "Well, sir, I don't mean to rush off, but I really need to be makin' tracks in a hurry."

"So long!" Julie shouted as the horse trader buried his spurs deep into the flanks of his mount and went galloping north with his string of horses trailing along behind.

"He was dirty," Julie said, "but he seemed real nice."

Longarm watched the rider disappear. "My guess is that he's a wanted man. Otherwise, why would he look like he'd just seen a ghost when I told him that I was a marshal?"

"Oh, he's probably just got a family; he's anxious to see his friends and family," Julie said. "Must you always be so suspicious?"

"Yes, because it keeps me alive," Longarm answered. "There's an old corral over there by that water tank. Let's walk these animals over that way and give them a drink. I'll need to shorten your stirrups before you ride, and I can do that while the horses drink their fill of water."

"All right."

Longarm led the horses to water and then asked, "Julie, are you much of a horseback rider?"

"I've never ridden in my life. And I'll be real honest with you . . . I'm scared to death of horses."

Longarm groaned. "Why didn't you tell me that before I bought you this Indian pony?"

"Because I was afraid you'd send me back and I really want to see the Grand Canyon."

"You won't have any problems with this little fella," Longarm assured her as he tightened her cinch. "This is a Navajo Indian pony. He's small and he's old. I expect he is also slow and lazy. You'll probably wear yourself out trying to keep up with me."

"Good."

"But he might be sneaky," Longarm added, looking into the pony's eyes and noting for the first time how his

35

ears were laid back hard against his ugly black head.

"Why don't you ride him around this corral a few times before I try him," Julie suggested.

"He's awful small for me," Longarm said. "And I've just shortened the stirrups."

"You can lengthen them again."

Longarm was in a hurry to be on their way, but he supposed that he ought to ride the pony before letting Julie up in her saddle. Satisfied that the cinch was on tight, he gripped the pony's bit and growled into its ear, "I'm going to ride you around this corral a couple of times, and you'd better behave yourself."

Without any more hesitation, Longarm rammed his boot into the stirrup and took his seat in the saddle. Suddenly, the Navajo pony ducked his head and started bucking furiously. Longarm grabbed the horn and tried to get his right foot into the off stirrup but failed.

"Hang on, honey!" Julie shouted.

Longarm was hanging on. But the little pony was so small and quick he felt as if he were riding a greased pig. Moments later, the Navajo pony reared, then sucked backward and sent Longarm over his head to crash into the pole fence. The pony snickered then trotted over to the center of the corral and watched as Longarm crawled weakly to his feet, clinging to the corral fence and cussing under his breath.

"I'm not going to ride that little demon!" Julie cried. "No sir! I'll walk first."

Longarm limped over to the pony, who made no attempt to run away. "We're going to do this again," he said, drawing his gun and pushing the Colt's barrel into the pony's ear. "And if you buck me off a second time, I'm going to blow what few brains you have all over this corral!"

The pony's eyes rolled around in their sockets. He snorted and then nodded his head up and down a few times. Longarm glanced over at a very nervous looking

Julie and said, "We've just had a little talk and we now have an understanding. He'll be fine this time."

"I hope so! He really threw you for a loop."

Longarm jammed his gun into his holster, then his boot into the stirrup. He shortened his reins so that the pony could not drop its head, and then he stepped on board and settled down firmly into the Indian saddle. The pony stood as still as a granite statue. Longarm waited tensely for the animal to try to buck again, and when he did not, Longarm finally relaxed and loosened the reins. The pony saw his chance. With a snort of defiance, he dropped his ugly little head and bucked with insane fury. Longarm had both boots planted firmly in their stirrups this time, but that made little difference. He lasted only six or seven jumps before the pony sent Longarm flying over that ugly head to smash into the corral posts a second time. He hit so hard the center pole cracked, and he was nearly knocked unconscious.

"Custis!" Julie shrieked, rushing to his side as the Navajo pony trotted back to the center of the corral to watch, ears flicking back and forth with curiosity.

Longarm turned his eyes north, glaring at the spot on the horizon where the horse trader had vanished. Then he turned his attention back to the corral. The pony was watching him closely, ears pointed forward. Longarm hissed, "I'm going to *shoot* him."

"No, please!"

"I'm going to do it, dammit!"

Longarm dragged himself erect. He reached for his gun, but Julie had already dragged it from his holster and now she ran off a little ways.

"Come back here and give me that gun!" Longarm shouted.

"I won't let you shoot him. He's . . . he's too cute!"

" 'Cute?' Is that what you said?" Longarm muttered with disbelief.

"That's right. Custis, I'd never be able to forgive you if you shot that poor little horse."

"He's a killer!"

"He's . . . well," Julie stuttered, ". . . he's probably just been mistreated. He needs to be loved."

"Shot!"

"Loved," she insisted.

"I'm not getting on him again and neither are you," Longarm vowed, never taking his eyes off the pony.

"Then we'll tie our bedrolls onto his back and I'll lead him into the Arizona Territory."

Julie was serious. "All right. We'll just do that," Longarm snapped.

All the rest of that day Julie led the Navajo pony along, and he seemed just as docile as a puppy. But by the time they reached Lee's Ferry, where they needed to cross the Colorado, Julie was exhausted.

"Over there," Longarm said as he drew his gun and fired it twice into the late afternoon sky, "lives a big Mormon family. Pretty soon they'll send a raft across this river and ferry us back over to their side."

Julie eyed the swift Colorado River nervously. "The raft won't overturn, will it?"

"Naw."

"What if the horses refuse to get on board?"

"Then I'll shoot them both and send them downriver for the fish to eat," Longarm joked.

Julie didn't find his remark one bit humorous. "You sure are quick to go to your gun, Custis. My heavens! You just killed three men in Silver Creek. And now, first little trouble we have and you talk about shooting two perfectly good horses."

"*One* good horse," Longarm corrected, patting the neck of his buckskin. "That Indian pony isn't even worth a bullet."

"You'd better not even think of it," Julie warned. "I

love you, Custis, but I can't abide a man who is cruel to poor animals."

"Yeah, well what about my back that he almost broke?" Longarm touched the small of his back and it still brought a wince of pain. "I didn't start the trouble, that pony did."

"That may be so, but that's no reason to kill the poor sweetheart."

Longarm wanted to throw up, because the pony was pure poison. No wonder the Navajo had gotten rid of the damned thing.

"There they are!" Julie cried, pointing across the river at a man and several children who came down to their big raft. "Do you know the name of this family?"

"Lee was the first family to settle and farm here, but I expect this is a different bunch."

"Look at all those lovely children. There are five of them and they're all waving." Julie waved and said, "Come on, Custis, don't be unfriendly. Wave back at them."

Longarm waved, but his heart wasn't in it. He was still fuming over having gotten cheated by the horse trader.

"Here they come!" Julie shouted. "How exciting."

Longarm forgot about his annoyance with the pony, although it galled him terribly to have been cheated. However, now his attention was fixed on the big raft that was being poled across the swift Colorado not only by the man, but also by several of his older children. Because of the strong current, the raft had started much farther up-river and, as Longarm watched, he could see the family straining to bring the raft into a small beach on their side of the water.

When the raft finally landed, Longarm went up to the pony and covered his eyes with a bandana. "Let's lead the horses down and take them right on board."

The pony didn't like being blindfolded, but when Longarm grabbed it by the bit and half dragged it forward, the little horse came along.

"Hello there!" the Mormon shouted. "Bring them horses right on board."

Longarm got the pony onto the raft, but the little animal snorted and its hooves danced nervously on the log planking. "This pony might just jump overboard. If he does, let him sink or swim."

"I sure will," the Mormon said, wiping sweat from his brow. "I've got too big a family to feed to risk my life for a sorry-looking pony."

"He's not sorry looking," a girl of about ten with long blonde pigtails and freckles all over her face argued. "Daddy, he's a *pretty* pony."

Her brothers rolled their eyes up to let everyone know they didn't share their little sister's opinion. The father just grinned. "He looks like an Indian pony with that Navajo saddle."

"He is," Longarm said. "And I'm not ashamed to admit that I really got skinned buying him from a horse trader. He didn't give me his name, but he was a tall, skinny fella with a gold tooth."

"I know that man," the Mormon said. "I've ferried him and his horses across this river many times. He's not to be trusted."

"I wish I'd known that earlier," Longarm said. He led the buckskin on board, and the two oldest boys pushed the raft back into the current.

Julie grabbed Longarm and held on tight as the big log raft was spun completely around by the current. The man and his sons poled hard, and it was easy to see that they knew their business. The Colorado was swift here, but not especially deep. Lee's Crossing, or Ferry as it was called, was about the only place to cross the river for several hundred miles in either direction.

"This is a great river," Longarm told Julie. "It's the lifeblood of the Southwest. Born above Denver in the highest part of the Rockies, it doesn't stop until it reaches the Gulf of Mexico."

"You're right about that!" the Mormon shouted over the crashing of the raft. "And there are times in the spring during the flood season when we won't even attempt to make this crossing. But she's passable now!"

The man was tall and rangy with a long, scraggly beard. Like his grinning sons, he was dressed poorly, and it was obvious that the family was not getting rich either farming the narrow canyon land leading north from the river, or in this river-crossing business. Perhaps, Longarm thought, they were also sending a good bit of their income to Mormon families even less fortunate than themselves. Mormons were very good about helping out one another, and Longarm had never known any of them to starve as long as they were willing to work.

When the raft finally touched the north shore, the pony didn't wait to be led, but ran blindly off the raft. His short legs were not nearly long enough to touch bottom, and he was nearly swept down the river by the current before managing to drag itself back to shore. By then, two of the farmer's boys had grabbed his bridle and reins and were leading him back to the raft.

"Almost lost him that time," the man said, tossing his pole into the weeds and wiping the sweat from his brow.

"Wouldn't have been much of a loss," Longarm replied.

"Sure it would have!" Julie protested.

"I take it you have no use for that pony," the oldest of the boys dared to say.

"No, I don't," Longarm told him. "It's a vicious bucker who can't be trusted."

The boy, whom Longarm judged to be about twelve, handed Longarm back his bandana and said, "I bet I could ride him."

"Liam!" the father said sharply. "Do not be forward or boastful."

"That's all right," Longarm said. "Boy, if you can ride this horse I would sell him to your father very cheap."

41

"How cheap?"

"Ten dollars," Longarm said, thinking it would be in his own best interests to cut his losses and buy Julie a better horse. Maybe even here if this Mormon farmer had a few for sale.

"He isn't worth that much," the farmer said.

"He is when you consider that he comes with a saddle, bridle, blanket and lead rope."

The Mormon ran his hands down the pony's legs to see if there were any knots or bowed tendons. Any sign of lameness. Finding none, he said, "Mister, I would give you seven dollars if Liam finds the horse agreeable."

"He won't," Longarm predicted. "And I'm warning you and him right now that that ugly old pony can really buck."

"Liam," the father said. "Check the cinch and the length of those stirrups. Then mount the pony and ride him around before we pay this man seven dollars."

"He won't let you ride him," Longarm warned. "I never saw such a bad bucker."

Liam wasn't listening. He tightened the cinch, shortened the stirrups and then rubbed the pony's muzzle for a moment, saying something to the animal that was too low and quiet to be heard.

"We're going to do fine," Liam said to Longarm with a shy but confident grin.

"You be careful!" Longarm shouted, grabbing Julie and pulling her clear of the pony. "First thing he'll do is get his head down, and then he'll . . ."

The Mormon boy wasn't listening. Ignoring the stirrups, he leapt onto the pony's back, kicked it with his bare heels, and went trotting off toward his family's house, barns and fields.

"Well I'll be damned!" Longarm swore.

"Please," the Mormon said with a pained expression. "I can't abide cursing, nor can any of my family."

"Excuse me. I'm so shocked that I forgot my manners. How . . . how in blazes did he do that?"

"Liam has a special way with horses, mules, and burros. They all like and trust him. I'll pay you for that pony and we'll keep him around for a while. We don't have a pony right now so he'll be good for my youngest children to ride when they go up into the red rock canyons to collect firewood and look for stray cattle."

But Longarm shook his head. "Liam might be good with that horse, but I sure wouldn't trust him with—"

"Would you look at that!" Julie cried. "He's coming back with two more riding him!"

Longarm stared in disbelief. Sure enough, Liam was in the front and two of his siblings were tucked close in behind, and neither one of them could have been more than five years old.

"He's a nice little Indian pony," the Mormon said, digging into his pants and dragging out a wad of wet bills. "Seven dollars is a fair price. I can sell that saddle, bridle, nice bit and blanket for five dollars so the pony is only costing me two dollars. I think that is a good and fair price for the animal by itself."

Longarm took the money even though he felt like he'd again gotten the short end of the stick.

"Would you like to stay the night for supper and rest?" the Mormon asked sounding hopeful. "Cost you only one dollar each for food and another dollar to feed and board that handsome buckskin."

Longarm was eager to be on his way to Gunshot, but he knew that Julie was too tired to go even a few more miles. "We'll stay. Is there a settlement anywhere around here?"

The man frowned. "The nearest one is called Faith, and it is about forty miles north."

"Does it have a hotel?" Julie asked.

"Oh no." The farmer smiled. "But it does have a general store and several houses where you could board."

"How far is Gunshot from here?" Longarm asked.

The Mormon's eyes narrowed. "Is that where you are headed?"

"Yes."

"With your wife," he asked, looking troubled.

"No," Longarm said, deciding it would be better among these people just to let them assume that he and Julie were married. "I have some business in Gunshot."

"Then it is bad business," the farmer said bluntly. "For that is a godless and evil place."

"I know that," Longarm said. "But I won't be there for very long. Right now, I need to leave my wife somewhere safe."

Julie looked at him curiously, but was wise enough to remain silent.

"Your wife could stay here and she would be safe."

"How far is it from here to Gunshot?" Longarm asked a second time.

"About one hundred miles."

"Excuse us," Longarm said, taking Julie aside where they could talk privately.

"Why did you lie to the man about me being your wife?"

"Because, if I hadn't, he'd have thought you a sinful woman. Julie, out here you are either married to the man you are with or you are living in sin. Which would you prefer?"

"All right," she conceded. "But I really don't want to stay here. It's too hot and although these seem like very nice people, I'd go stir crazy in this canyon."

"I understand." Longarm was beginning to regret having allowed Julie to come this far, but he was determined that they make the best of things.

"You could stay in Faith," he told her.

"Why don't we go there and take a look," she answered.

44

"All right. I'll have to buy you a horse . . . if they have any for sale."

"Can't we ride double for forty miles?"

"If we have to," he told her. "But that sure isn't my preference."

Longarm went over to the Mormon farmer and said, "I think we'll go on to Faith tomorrow. Do you have any horses for sale that my wife can ride?"

"I'm afraid not."

"Then we'll ride double."

"That buckskin is a fine animal, but the road to Faith is almost all uphill through the rock country. It will be hard on your horse."

"We have no choice."

"She could stay," the farmer repeated. "Only one dollar a day until your return. We would not expect her to do any family chores."

"I understand," he said. "But she wants to come with me. And she wants to visit the Grand Canyon."

"I see. Very well."

The man went inside his house, which was made of adobe and looked solid. A moment later, he beckoned for Longarm and Julie to come inside and meet his wife and their smallest children. The wife's name was Margaret and she had two healthy infants.

"We are sorry that you cannot stay with us longer," the plump, red-cheeked woman told them. "But I understand. This is not a good place for a woman who has not been raised to endure the heat and the isolation."

"Is Faith a nice town?"

"It is a very small farming and ranching community," she said, looking at Julie. "Good families live there. You will be well treated."

Longarm sure hoped so. He was beginning to think he was a terrible fool to have allowed Julie to come this far.

But then again, she had been a pleasure to know and to love and he was determined that, when the trouble was over in Gunshot, he would take her to see the magnificent Grand Canyon.

Chapter 5

The Mormon family living at Lee's Ferry, or Cozy Dell as the missus preferred to call it, wished Longarm and Julie well the following morning when they prepared to ride on to Faith, Utah. Liam and several of his sisters rode the Navajo pony to accompany Longarm and Julie for about a mile before they stopped to say good-bye.

"I'm glad that you now own that pony," Julie told the Mormon boy. "Mr. Long was close to shooting him yesterday."

Liam and his sisters were obviously shocked.

"Why?" one of the little girls asked, looking at Custis as if he were a monster.

"Because that pony bucked him off."

"Twice," Longarm grated, still feeling the pain.

"He did that," the smallest girl said, "because you are way too big for him to carry. Don't you know that, mister?"

Longarm couldn't help but grin. "I'm sure that you're right. We'll see you children again when we come back through and need to cross the Colorado River."

"Be careful," Liam told them, looking far too serious for a boy so young. "My father says that there are some bad men in Gunshot. Men who have no fear of God."

"We'll be careful," Longarm promised a moment before he sent the buckskin climbing north up the rutted road.

The sun was hot and the land was parched, but as they traveled north into higher country, they were greeted by spectacular rock formations. Some looked like copper toadstools, others were jagged spires backdropped by spectacular vermilion cliffs reaching up to a clear, azure sky.

"I've never seen a country so stark and yet so beautiful," Julie said. "It looks like Satan's playground."

"Oh, it's magnificent country, all right," Longarm agreed. "It's so huge and empty that it can make you feel small."

"Even you?" she asked, hugging his waist and laying her head against his broad back as they rode along.

"Sure, even me," he told her. "This is still largely unexplored country. It's always been the home of the Navajo, Paiute, and Ute Indians and they've not always been the friendliest people toward whites. Why, it's been less than thirty years since Major John Wesley Powell first came through the Grand Canyon on wooden boats."

"Why are all those vultures floating around in circles up ahead of us?" Julie asked.

"That means that something is either dead or dying."

"What could it be?"

"Probably an old cow or a sheep," Longarm said. "Might be something as small as a rabbit or maybe even a deer or mountain goat that has gotten weak and is about to die. We'll find out soon enough."

"Those sure are ugly birds."

"They have their function to serve," Longarm replied. "They clean up carrion. Pick a carcass right down to the bones."

"Ugh!"

Longarm leaned forward to help their buckskin labor

up the steep, dusty road toward Faith and whatever the turkey vultures were about to devour.

"Will they pick at a dying animal?" Julie asked.

"If it's small and weak enough. But they're patient birds. They know that everything dies in time."

"I wouldn't mind it if you shoot them out of the sky."

"No sense in making them pay for what they were put on earth to do," Longarm told her. "And besides, I don't even have a rifle. They're way out of pistol range."

"They give me the shivers," Julie said.

"Well, we ought to be able to see what they're after when we top this ridge," Longarm told her as his horse strained up the last few yards to the summit of a long, twisting road.

When the heavily breathing animal finally topped the rise, they looked down to see a sight that made the hair of Longarm's neck stand up and quiver.

"Oh my god!" Julie cried. "What are those men—"

Longarm wheeled their horse around and sent it galloping back down the road they'd just climbed. Now well back from view, he reined the animal up and helped Julie to the ground before he also dismounted.

"What were those men doing?" Julie whispered.

"They are raping two women," Longarm said, his face grim. "Did you see the three bodies lying beside that burning, covered wagon?"

Julie nodded. "Did those horrible men see us?"

"I don't think so," Longarm told her. "At least I hope not."

"What are we going to do!"

Longarm drew his six-gun and moved back toward the crown of the ridge. He glanced back over his shoulder. "Julie, just stay put and keep quiet."

Longarm crept up to the top of the ridge and peered ahead into a valley choked by sagebrush and ringed by red rocks. His first impression had been correct. Four men were having their way with two women, whose long

49

dresses were bunched up around their waists.

The distance was too great to see details, but from the carnage around the burning wagon, Longarm was quite certain that this had been a pair of immigrant families traveling in a single covered wagon. The wagon's team of mules were tied off in the brush accompanied by a milk cow and four saddled horses. Longarm counted three dead men lying facedown out in the brush. His first impulse was to leap into his saddle and charge down with his gun blazing.

And then he thought about Julie and realized that not only would he be outnumbered, he would be facing men who had rifles while all he had was a Colt revolver. A charge would be suicide and then what would happen to Julie?

Longarm swore in helpless silence. *Think this through. Don't pull a George Armstrong Custer and throw your life away, and that of Julie's as well, for nothing! Think!*

But the sight of four men using two poor women, whose husbands and sons had just been murdered, filled Longarm with a quiet, killing rage. After a few moments, he hurried back to Julie.

She threw herself into his arms crying, "What can we do to help those poor women!"

"I'm thinking on it," he said.

"You can't just go flying over the hill," she told him. "Custis, they'd shoot you out of the saddle."

"I know."

"Then . . ."

Longarm closed his eyes for a moment, concentrating hard. "We have to get them to come after us."

"I don't understand."

He opened his eyes. "Julie, there's only one way that I can think of to help those women, and that's to create a distraction."

"But—"

He grabbed her by the shoulders. "Listen to me. You

need to get on our horse and ride over the top of that rise and then start down toward them. When they realize that you're a woman, they'll come after you in a rush."

"All of them?"

"I hope so," he said. "Ride back over the top of the rise, and I'll be waiting to shoot them out of their saddles."

Julie hugged him tightly. "What if they kill you instead?"

"That's the chance we take. Either that, or we ride away from this and leave those two women to a terrible fate, and frankly, I don't think that's something either of us can do in good conscience."

"I'm afraid."

"I'm kind of worried myself," he admitted knowing that, if he were killed, three women were probably going to die before the sun set this evening. "But there's no other way."

Julie lifted her chin. "All right. How far do I ride ahead?"

"Not far. All that's necessary is that they see you and realize that you're a woman. That ought to do it. I'll be waiting to ambush them the moment they come into view. Besides my forty-four forty, I also carry that hidden two-shot derringer."

"But you can't hit anything at a distance with a derringer."

"That's why I'll wait until they are right on top of me," Longarm told her. "Julie, can you do this?"

"I will because I have to."

"Good girl!"

Longarm helped her into the saddle, saying, "You don't have to ride very fast over the rise. Keep the buckskin under control and moving forward at a steady walk. Just don't let him stop until they see you, and then wait for them to give chase. When they do, ride fast back over the rise and keep going past me."

Longarm placed his hand on her thigh. "Julie, you can't stop or look back when you ride past me. If I'm shot, it will only be after I have killed several of them first. If any remain, they might be wounded and unable to chase you back to Lee's Ferry."

"But that's miles behind us!"

"Downhill," he reminded her. "And this buckskin will be carrying only one light rider, so you'll have a good chance of escaping even if the very worst happens to me."

"But—"

Longarm didn't want to hear her protestations. He gave the buckskin a firm swat on the rump, sending the big horse forward with Julie clinging to the saddle horn. Then he followed her to the rise, dropped to the ground, and drew his six-gun.

The four outlaws were so preoccupied with their helpless victims that they didn't see Julie riding down the hill toward them until she was just three hundred yards away. Then one of the men who was waiting his turn looked up and his jaw dropped.

Rein in the horse and get ready to come back in a hurry, Longarm thought, his Colt clenched in his right hand and his back-up derringer ready in his left hand. *Come on girl, you can do this!*

"Hey!" the outlaw bellowed. "Look, another woman!"

The two men who were pleasuring themselves twisted around while the fourth man stood, gawking.

"Now," Longarm whispered. "They've seen enough to know you're young and you're pretty! Come on back, Julie."

As if she could hear his orders, Julie reined the buckskin around and, still clutching the saddle horn as if it were a lifeline in the hands of a drowning man, she sent the big horse into a gallop.

"Get her!" one of the rapists shouted.

The two that were standing raced for their mounts. They were young and they were quick. In only a few

52

moments, they were charging after Julie, whipping their horses and urging them forward at a hard run.

Longarm remained spread-eagled on the ground a dozen yards off to one side of the road, with only the crown of his snuff-brown hat revealing his presence. He rested the barrel of his Colt revolver across his left forearm, knowing that he had to kill this pair and then hope that the two remaining men did not murder the women they'd been abusing before he could rescue them. It would have suited him far more if they'd all taken up the chase and tried to ride Julie down.

Julie was bouncing all over the saddle and the buckskin was giving it his best effort, but the tall horse was fading quickly due to the double weight he'd been carrying. Suddenly, however, the big horse burst over the top of the ridge and went galloping down the steep road back toward Lee's Ferry. Longarm caught a glimpse of the Denver office girl's face, and it was frozen with fear.

He took a deep breath and cussed himself for not having bought a rifle. He would have if he hadn't spent so much time and money fooling with Julie. Now, that earlier dalliance might just cost him his life.

It was hard, but Longarm waited until the pair of riders burst over the crown of the ridge and then he opened fire, shooting one out of the saddle with his first bullet, but missing the second. If the rider had kept on going after Julie, he might have gotten away with his life. But the fool reined up in surprise, then drew his gun and charged at Longarm, who had sat up and now steadied his gun on his bent knees.

"Come on!" he said as the horseman opened fire, spraying harmless bullets into the brush.

It was as easy as shooting a fish in a barrel. Longarm steadied his aim and pulled the trigger. His first slug struck the rider dead center in his chest. The man made a vain attempt to grab his saddle horn and Longarm shot him a second time, his bullet a little high so that it tore open the rider's throat. The rapist tumbled from his saddle, only instead of falling free, the man's boot got hung up in his stirrup.

Longarm sprang to his feet and raced to grab the now riderless horse, but it swept past him and back over the hill.

It was the worst thing that could have happened. Now the two men down in the valley watched their lifeless friend being dragged down the road toward them.

"Damn!" Longarm swore.

He looked back south and Julie was still riding hard toward Lee's Ferry, just as he'd ordered. But the horse that had been ridden by the first man he'd killed had stopped and was now standing on its reins, snorting and looking uncertain as to its next move. And jammed under its saddle was a Winchester carbine.

Longarm needed that horse. Needed him bad.

Forcing himself to keep calm, he started walking toward the horse. He expected that the last two killers down in the valley might execute the women they'd been abusing, but that was beyond his control. All he could do now was to try and get this horse and the carbine. If he could do that, he was almost on an equal footing with the final two men that he intended to kill.

"Easy," he said, trying to keep his voice calm and relaxed. "Take it easy now."

The riderless horse shied away in terror and just when Longarm felt certain that it was going to run, the animal again stepped on its reins and brought itself up short.

"Easy, boy."

The bay gelding snorted, rolled its eyes, and watched Longarm approach. "There," Longarm said, grabbing up the reins and patting the gelding a moment before he slid the Winchester free and levered in a shell.

He could hear shouts and racing hoofbeats.

They're coming to investigate. Good.

Longarm knew he only had a few precious minutes

before the two riders burst over the top of the ridge. But that was all the time he needed. He tied the horse to a bush, then moved away from the animal and raised the Winchester to his shoulder. The good news was that his aim was where they would appear, and he would have them instantly in his sights. The bad news was that he'd never fired this rifle before and every weapon shot a little differently. Maybe to one side or the other or high or low.

For a moment, he considered using his pistol again. It had worked well only moments ago. But he decided to stick with the Winchester. It had more killing power and range should either of the two riders sweep past him and go racing after Julie.

Steady now.

The first horseman that came into view was much older than Longarm expected. His beard was gray and it was tobacco stained near the corners of his mouth. The top of his head was bald, but the long hair that covered his ears was silver. He was big and he was fat.

When he came flying over the ridge, he had a gun in his fist and was screaming curses and the name of what was either his friend or maybe even his dead son. "Monk! Monk!"

Then he saw Longarm and the Winchester swinging to take aim at his chest. The man had tried to bring his pistol to bear on Longarm just as a rifle slug tore into his huge belly. He howled and somehow unleashed a wild shot. Missing, he tried to run Longarm down with his horse.

Longarm had to throw himself sideways or he would have been knocked flying. And while he rolled and jumped back to his feet, the fat man was still in the saddle and trying desperately to turn his mount around and again charge Longarm.

The man made a big, easy target, and Custis shot him between his humped shoulders. The old rapist lifted up in his stirrups and reached for the sky as if beseeching

55

heaven. Longarm had no mercy and drilled him again, this time low in the spine.

The big man screamed, fell, and rolled over and over like a log. His horse raced on down the road after Julie, but Longarm didn't have time to watch because the last of the killers was already over the ridge and emptying his six-gun.

Longarm felt a bullet crease his left arm. He steadied his aim, fired twice and was on target both times. The last rider slumped over in his saddle and swept past. Longarm took aim, but the man tumbled out of his saddle before Longarm could fire again.

It was over.

Longarm reloaded his Colt, then walked toward the old man, who was somehow alive enough to keep thrashing about in the brush. Longarm cautiously approached the dying man and, deciding that he posed no threat, stood over him and demanded, "Who are you?"

The fat man's porcine lips moved silently and his round, bearded face contorted in a supreme effort. "Go . . . to . . . hell!"

"No," Longarm said, "that's reserved for you murders and rapists."

"Shoot . . . me!"

If the old man had been a wounded animal, Longarm would not have hesitated in putting him out of his misery. It was clear that the killer was dying and equally clear that he was paralyzed from the waist down. His eyes held a silent plea, but Longarm turned his back on the old man and went to check on the other three outlaws. He was taking no chances that one of them was still alive and might have the strength to rise up and kill him with his last dying breath.

But they were all dead. Longarm could still hear the fat man choking and gasping. It was hard to ignore those sounds and, in some deep part of him, he had to give the man credit for his strength and will to live. But on another level, he wished he could torture him for what he and his three companions had done to the people who had been traveling with the covered wagon.

"You're taking this pretty hard," he said, standing over the man and gazing down into his now graying face. "If you tell me who you and the others are, maybe I'll be good enough to send word to your family."

The offer was received with spewing venom and profanity. The fat man almost managed to grab Longarm's leg. Jumping back, Longarm said, "I guess that means you're not interested in being buried, huh?"

He gazed up at the turkey vultures still circling in the sky. "I'm going to let them pick your bones clean, old man. I'll bury the travelers you killed and I'll try to save the women you raped, but I'll be damned if I will save your rotting carcass from the coyote and the buzzards. Was Monk your son?"

The old man tried to spit at him, but the spittle didn't get past his face. A glob of it hung in his beard. Longarm shook his head and said, "I've felt worse about killing a rattlesnake than I do about killing you and your son, Monk. He was your son, wasn't he?"

The old man gave one last try at rising and then he fell back, dead.

Longarm trudged over to the tied horse, mounted, and rode past the old man, who stared at him with blank but still hate-filled eyes. Then he set the horse into a gallop over the top of the rise and on down toward the two women, who were now bent over their own dead.

Longarm drew his horse up to a stop, and when one of the women jumped up and took off running, he shouted, "I won't hurt you! I'm a United States marshal. I mean you no harm!"

The woman spun around and stared back at him. Then she crumpled to the ground sobbing.

Longarm turned to gaze back toward the ridge, wishing that he could see Julie coming down to help. She'd be better with these women than himself. She'd be able to help them . . . if they weren't already far beyond human help.

He dismounted and went over to the brown-haired woman. She might have been young, but he couldn't be sure because her face was a mass of bruises, swollen and misshapen from the beating and abuse she'd endured.

"It's alright," he said, instantly wishing he could take back those stupid words because it wasn't alright. "Who are you?"

She had long, brown hair, and now she brushed it back from her eyes. "I am Mrs. Huddle. That man," she said pointing to a body, "is Mr. Huddle."

"Who is the other woman?"

"Mrs. Evans. She lost both her husband and her son."

"We're going to take care of you," Longarm told her, reaching out his hand.

The woman recoiled in fear. "How do I know you're not . . . one of them?"

"Because I wear this." He reached into his pocket and showed her his badge. "Where you heading?"

"For New Mexico. We were going to resettle there."

"Are you Mormon?"

"No."

"There is a place back a ways called Lee's Ferry. We're going to take you there and see if we can get you ladies some help."

She nodded, but her expression was so distracted that Longarm was not at all sure the woman understood. Then she walked back to her fallen husband and collapsed by his side.

Longarm went over to the woman's son. The kid was tall and slender. He was lying facedown and his head was bloody. He clutched an old cap-and-ball revolver in his fist. Longarm removed and inspected the weapon, noting that it had been fired three times before jamming. At least the kid had put up a fight before being cut down in the prime of his life. Rolling the kid over, Longarm crouched on his haunches and studied the boy's face. He had sandy hair and he had been handsome. What a shame that he'd. . . .

The young man's fingers twitched as if trying to regain his revolver. Longarm grabbed his wrist and there was definitely a pulse. "Hey," he shouted, "this young fella is still alive!"

Mrs. Evans let out a shout and came running. By the time she arrived, Longarm had the kid cradled in his arms and he was inspecting the head wound. "He's shot, but the bullet may not have penetrated his brain. I have a feeling that it just looks worse than it is. Ma'am, we need to get your son back to Lee's Ferry and see if he can pull through this injury."

"Praise the Lord!" the poor woman cried, falling to her knees and raising her hands to the sky.

Longarm tried to rouse the young man, but he was unconscious. The bullet that had struck his head had knocked him out, and it was impossible to tell what kind of shape he was really in right now.

"Are you saying that my Henry might live!"

"That's exactly what I'm saying. His pulse is weak but steady. You can see that he's lost a lot of blood. But ma'am, I've seen more than my share of head wounds and I'd say your boy has a fair chance of pulling through if we can get him doctored up."

Mrs. Evans wiped tears from her eyes. "Please don't give me false hope. My heart will break if I lose both of them."

Longarm examined the head wound more carefully. "It's just a crease. A deep one, but only a crease, and I don't think the bullet penetrated the skull."

"Henry and his father are thick headed."

"Ma'am. Right now I need some water to wash his face and head, then something to use as a bandage. Can you get me water and a bandage?"

Mrs. Evans's own face was bloodied, and he knew that she was racked with pains. But that didn't seem to matter as she scurried away while Longarm knelt beside her son.

"You're going to pull through this," he told the kid. "It appears to me that you are all that your dear mother has left in this world. She needs you, so don't let her down."

Henry's mother was back in just a few moments. Longarm let her wash her son's face and bandage his head. He went over to Mrs. Huddle and asked, "Who were those four men?"

"I don't know. At first they acted friendly. We invited them to share our meal, and that's when they drew their guns and shot my-my husband. Then . . ." The woman burst into sobs, unable to continue.

"I'm sorry," he told her. "I wish I had come sooner."

Longarm left the woman and walked slowly over to stand apart from the burning wagon. There were some clothes and trunks that had been torn out of the wagon, and their contents lay scattered in the dirt and the brush. These things needed to be collected. He would shake the clothes out and pack them into the trunks while the widows grieved over their husbands. Then they would round up the horses, drape the dead over their saddles, and start off toward the river as fast as they could in order to save Henry Evans.

"Custis!"

He looked up to see Julie galloping down from the ridge. She was bouncing high in the saddle and the buckskin was covered with white lather. From the looks of the poor horse, Julie had let it run for miles, until it stopped just short of dying.

This is a hell of a country, he thought, glancing up at the vultures. *And you ugly birds are going to have four bodies to feed upon before the sun goes down.*

Chapter 6

It was a long and sad ride back to Lee's Ferry with the two grieving women and the bodies of their husbands. Henry Evans was still out cold and Longarm had to hold him upright in his saddle while riding double behind. Every few miles, Henry groaned, and that was music to their ears.

"How much farther!" his mother kept asking.

"Not too much farther," Longarm would reply, even though the distance was considerable. "How old is this kid?"

"He's eighteen. My only son. He's much like his . . . his father." Mrs. Evans burst into fresh tears. "Why would anyone do something like that to us!"

Julie was riding double with the poor woman and doing everything she could to raise her spirits. The younger widow, Mrs. Rebecca Huddle, seemed to be lost in her own dark thoughts. She rode side by side next to the horse that carried the body of her husband. Now and then she would reach out and touch the dead man and then try to keep from sobbing.

Longarm had seen plenty of grieving mothers and widows, but this was as sad a situation as he could remember. In a few days, if it didn't rain hard, he'd come back to the site of the rapes and murders and see if he could pick up the trail that the killers had made before they'd intercepted the Huddle and Evans families. And if he was able to do that, he'd be willing to bet that trail would lead him to Gunshot.

This is going to make bringing that bunch to justice even sweeter, he thought as the long miles passed on their way back to Lee's Ferry.

It was at least midnight when they finally made it back to the Colorado River and Cozy Dell. Longarm hailed the Wilson's house and it blazed with lamplight a few moments later. Then Mr. Wilson, a rifle in his hand, came outside in his nightgown.

"Who goes there!" he shouted, raising the weapon and pointing it loosely in their direction.

"It's Custis Long! We've got wounded and dead and we need help."

Mrs. Wilson hurried outside along with Liam and the younger children to watch the procession file into their yard.

Caleb and his wife took the entire situation in at a glance and quickly took charge. "Mr. Long," he said, "we'll take your horses around behind the barn. The ladies can come inside."

Longarm dismounted and then eased Henry out of his saddle. "We've got a wounded young man here. I'll carry him into the house."

More lanterns were lit and soon they had Henry on a bed. Longarm checked his pulse one more time. "It's holding steady. I think he's got a good chance of making it."

"You run along now," the lady of the house said. "We'll be taking care of everything in here."

"Yes," Julie said. "We can handle it ourselves."

Longarm marched out of the house and to the barn where Caleb and young Liam were pulling the bodies of Mr. Huddle and Mr. Evans from the horses.

"What happened?" the Mormon asked, holding his lantern over the two dead men. "They've both been shot more than once."

"I doubt that they ever had a chance," Longarm said, looking at the farmer and his son. "From what I could learn, these two men, their wives and young Henry, who is wounded, were jumped by surprise by four men who first posed as being neighborly. I would imagine that the men were gunned down instantly."

"And women were . . ."

Longarm glanced at Liam. Even in the lamplight, he could see how pale and shaken the boy was. "The women were beaten," Longarm said, leaving it at that and knowing that the farmer would soon enough learn about the outrage that the two woman had suffered.

"And there was nothing you could do?" Caleb asked.

"No. The killings must have taken place quite some time before we came upon the scene. I left the four killers to feed the buzzards. One of them was named Monk. I killed him and his father, a big, fat man with a full gray beard stained yellow from tobacco. Do you know who they are?"

Caleb nodded. "They're part of the bunch that hole up at Gunshot. They're all outlaws, murderers and thieves. I wish death on no man, but it sounds like you had no choice."

"It wouldn't have been long before they'd have killed Mrs. Huddle and Mrs. Evans," Longarm said. "The only reason Henry Evans is alive is because his face and hair were covered with his own blood. They just figured he was dead and that is what saved his life."

"I sure hope the lad makes it," Caleb said, glancing at his own fine son. "Those animals deserved death!"

"We need to bury Mr. Huddle and Mr. Evans first thing tomorrow morning," Longarm said.

"Yes," the Mormon agreed. "I have picks and shovels and we have a little cemetery just out beyond the root cellar. It's fenced. The ground is hard, but we ought to get the graves dug by daybreak, if you're up to it. Be easier in the cool of the night."

"Then let's get it done with," Longarm said, not relishing the idea of digging graves in rocky ground. But there really was no choice. In this heat, the three bodies would decay quickly. They needed to be buried before they began to putrefy.

"I'll get more lanterns," Liam offered, hurrying back toward the house.

Caleb went into the dark barn and emerged a few minutes later carrying digging tools. He handed a shovel to Longarm saying, "I'll use the pick because my hands are already toughened for the hard work of breaking up ground. When I loosen it, you shovel it out."

"All right."

The Mormon studied him. "You killed four gunmen today. Four tough and deadly men."

"I had no choice."

"I know that." Caleb glanced toward the house for a moment, then looked back at Longarm. "Before my son Liam returns, I have to know something."

"You can ask."

"Mister, who *are* you?"

Longarm had promised himself that, when he got anywhere near Gunshot, he would assume the identity of the man on the wanted posters. However, given the circumstances, he decided it was wrong to be anything less than completely honest with this good family.

"I'm a United States deputy marshal sent here from Denver to stop the killing and outrages."

"One man?"

Longarm shrugged. "This is what I do."

"You have no idea of what you are up against."

"After today, I have a pretty good picture."

"Mr. Long, I do not mean to insult you, but one man

is not enough to make a change here. We need the United States Army."

"It may come to that," Longarm said. "But right now, I'm all that we've got."

"You'll be dead before you ever set foot in Gunshot."

"I'm going to pose as an outlaw and find out who is the ringleader."

"And who is the woman you brought with you? I want an honest answer."

"She isn't my wife."

"That much we had guessed. Why did you bring such a person to a place like this?"

"I've been asking myself the same question."

"If she is killed, it will be on your conscience." Caleb's mouth tightened in disapproval. "It was wrong to have brought her just for your own pleasure."

Although it sounded ridiculous given what they'd seen this day, Longarm told the truth. "Julie wouldn't be stopped from visiting the Grand Canyon."

"Foolishness! Send her back."

"I can't."

Wilson started to say more, but Liam arrived with a lantern in each fist. He stared at the bodies, then looked to his father and said, "The man is still unconscious but he's moaning now. Mother says that is a good sign."

"It is," Caleb said, taking one of the lanterns and starting off toward the family cemetery, leaving Longarm to follow.

He overtook the Mormon and said, "Listen, Mr. Wilson. Julie isn't going any farther than the settlement of Faith. After that, I'll go to Gunshot on my own."

"You're a walking dead man. We'll pray for you."

"I'm a passably good actor," Longarm replied. "And I'm no fool. If what I find in Gunshot is too much for me to handle, I'll send for help."

"How?" the Mormon asked. "There are no mail runs or

telegraph offices in Gunshot. How would you get word to the outside world if you need help?"

"I don't know yet." Longarm studied the man's face. "Can I count on your help?"

"No. I'm sorry, but you've seen the size of my family. I can't leave the missus to raise them alone if I were killed."

It was the answer that Longarm had expected. "I understand."

"But there are young men who have less responsibility than I do," Wilson said. "All of this Utah Territory was settled by Brigham Young and the faithful. We've been persecuted for our beliefs and practices. We've had to learn how to stand up for ourselves and fight . . . if necessary. I can only tell you this . . . what is happening in Gunshot is a disease that could spread if it is not exorcised."

"Are you saying that there are those among you that I could call upon to help?"

"That is exactly what I am saying."

"And how would I let them know if I need their help?"

"They would know," Wilson said a moment before walking off toward a little graveyard.

Longarm followed the tall, worn, and barefoot man over to the cemetery, which was protected from game and livestock by a wooden fence about three feet high. There were no less than ten grave markers, and all of them were made of wood and hand carved.

"Death is no stranger to this place," Wilson said. "Children have died of smallpox. People have drowned trying to cross the river without using the ferry. Two Paiutes were murdered for no reason whatsoever, and we buried them alongside our own."

Wilson moved off to one corner of the cemetery and swung his pick. Now Longarm really saw how hard the ground was because he saw a spark fly as iron bit into rock. It was going to be a long, backbreaking afternoon.

• • •

They worked until dusk but still were not finished. The graves were still much too shallow. Wilson was bathed in sweat and so was Longarm. He'd taken turns using the pick when the farmer had exhibited signs of exhaustion.

Longarm watched the upper rim of the canyon turn to fire. He studied the large and well tended but obviously suffering corn and vegetable gardens. "Tell me this, Caleb. Why do you stay here? Is it because you have been ordered to do so by Brigham Young?"

"Partly. But also because we are missionaries. Many people come here to cross the Colorado. For a very little price . . . and sometimes even for free . . . me and my family care for the weary, the sick, and the grieving. People like the two women you brought today. We mend their harness, fix their wagons, restore them both in mind and body. And, in our own quiet way, we tell them about our religious beliefs."

"Have you converted anyone to your church?"

"Oh yes! And even those who abide with their own faith leave this place with a new and better understanding of our church. In that way, we are doing God's work according to our beliefs."

"I see." Longarm chose his words carefully. "Have you or your friends ever had any trouble with the people at Gunshot?"

"We have. But nothing like what you bring to us today."

"Mr. Wilson?"

They turned to see Mrs. Wilson, who looked at the horses and bodies, then back to her husband. "It is not right to leave these bodies draped across the backs of horses. I think you should bring them over here and we ladies will prepare them for a proper burial."

"Yes," he said. "That would be good."

"But first," his wife said, "you must eat and rest."

"I am not hungry," he told her.

67

"You must eat anyway. Come to the house."

Longarm could see that the man was nearly exhausted, and he was not far behind. They did need to eat and rest for a while. The ground had not gotten any softer and they had been forced to use a sharp-pointed iron bar to pry some of the larger rocks out of the graves.

"Come," the woman said.

Julie met them halfway to the house. "Custis, you look terrible."

"I'll survive."

"Those poor widows are so sad."

"They have good reason."

"Yes. What will become of them now?"

"I don't know. But I have to go on to Gunshot. I'm sure that you can stay here until I return."

Julie craned her neck back and looked at the dark silhouettes of the canyon rim high above. I don't know if I can stand being here very long."

"Then I'll try to take care of business quickly and come back for you."

She hugged him tightly. "Young Evans has regained consciousness."

"That's the first good news I've heard in a while," Longarm said. "I'd better go talk to him. Maybe he can tell us something that his mother and Mrs. Huddle did not."

Longarm and Julie headed back to the little farmhouse. Henry was sitting up, and although he was pale, he was alert. Longarm judged him to be somewhere between eighteen and twenty years old.

He stood beside the young man's bed and asked, "How are you feeling?"

"Not too bad, sir."

Henry tried to stand but Longarm placed his hand on the man's shoulder. "These head injuries can take a while to heal. You lost a lot of blood and just need to take things easy."

Henry settled back and Longarm pulled up a chair. "You were pretty lucky to survive. I'm sure sorry that I can't say the same thing for your father and Mr. Huddle."

"I warned them not to trust those four men. And at first, we didn't. But the old one was smiling and seemed so nice that we let down our guard." Henry's eyes brimmed with tears. "And look what it cost us!"

Longarm wondered if the young man knew that his mother and Mrs. Huddle had been raped. Maybe not, and that would be a blessing.

"Henry, did your mother tell you what happened when I arrived?"

"Only that you somehow killed all four." Henry looked up at him. "And for that, I'll be forever grateful."

"It's my job, and I had a little help from Julie."

"Not much," she said.

"Enough." Longarm frowned. "Did the old man or any of the others say where they were from?"

"No, sir. And now, it seems kind of stupid that we didn't ask. They said they were looking for strays so we just naturally assumed they were of the Mormon faith and lived in this area. I realize now how wrong that was."

"Yes. Did they mention anything about the town of Gunshot?"

"We'd heard of it and my pa mentioned it but they said they had nothing to do with that bad bunch."

"Were there any others besides the four I killed?"

"No, sir. And, if you don't mind me askin', how did you do it?"

Longarm shrugged. "I had the element of surprise on my side. I nailed two of them when they charged over the hill and got the other two before they knew what was happening."

"You sure must be something with a gun."

"I manage," Longarm told the young man. "But killing is never something you want to brag about. Main thing is that you're going to be all right. Henry, your mother is going to need your help very much in the days and even the years to come."

"I know that." Henry's eyes burned with tears, which he angrily scrubbed dry. "I don't know what we're to do now that Pa is dead."

"You'll have time to figure it out," Longarm said. "Can you go back where you came from?"

"We could," Henry replied. "But we were all excited about movin' down to New Mexico. We had other friends there and they said they'd help us get a fresh start."

"Then that's probably what you should go on ahead and do," Longarm told the young man. "It's been my experience that you can't ever go back and expect things to be as they were. I made the mistake of trying that once . . . after the war."

"And you were sorry?"

"Yes," Longarm told him. "Everything I knew as a boy was destroyed by soldiers. I was sorry that I didn't just keep it all as a good memory in my mind."

"I got a mind to get strong again and learn to use a gun." Henry managed a smile. "All I am now is a farm kid. But I got bigger ideas in mind."

"Nothing wrong with farming. You'll live longer and better with a plow handle in your hand than a gun. Stick to what you know and to what your pa taught you and you'll never be sorry."

"Yes, sir, but I surely do admire what you did to them that killed my pa."

Longarm didn't have anything to say about that so he turned away and joined Caleb at the table.

"We'll eat and then sleep for an hour or two," the Mormon decided. "We ought to have the graves ready for the burying by sunup."

"I expect so," Longarm said. "And as soon as the dead are put to rest, I'll be on my way to Gunshot."

Caleb looked closely at him. "In that case, perhaps I

should just go ahead and dig a third grave for you, Marshal Long."

Henry overheard the comment and sat up. "Sir, are you really a United States marshal?"

"Yes I am," Longarm said, aware that everyone in the room was listening. "I've been sent from Denver to see what I can do about cleaning up Gunshot. To do that, I have to get in among those people, and the only way that can happen is if they think I'm also an outlaw. That's why it's so important that no one says anything to give away my true identity."

"No one will say a word," Caleb promised. "But I still say that you're heading for an early grave by going into that viper's den."

Custis didn't know how to respond to that pessimistic remark, so he dug into the food and avoided looking at Julie.

Chapter 7

They'd spent most of the night scratching out the graves so they'd be deep enough that wild animals would never dig up the corpses. At dawn, they laid the two men to rest with prayers and tears. Watching the widows made Longarm all the more determined to infiltrate the Gunshot Gang and to put an end to their bloody deprivations.

When the words had all been spoken and the tears shed, Longarm grabbed a long-handled shovel and, with blistered palms, helped Caleb cover the bodies. Afterward, everyone went back to the house and sat around looking desolated.

"I'd better saddle up and move on," Longarm finally announced, avoiding Julie's eyes. "The sooner I get to Gunshot the sooner I can find out how to stop this sort of thing."

"There's nothing that will stop it except to kill every last man that hides in that place," the Mormon said bitterly. "It's for certain that they are not going to listen either to you . . . or the word of God . . . and repent."

Longarm nodded and headed outside, with Julie close on his heels. He took her hand and they walked to the corral, where Longarm hooked his heel over the lower rail, turned to Julie, and said, "What do you want to do?

Stay here . . . or I can take you back up the trail to Faith."

She glanced back at the Mormon cabin. "I think I'd better stay here and lend support to those widows while they grieve."

"Probably the best thing to do," Longarm said in agreement. He ducked through the cedar corral poles, then bridled and saddled his tall buckskin. He led the animal outside and closed the corral gate and started to put his boot into the stirrup when Julie grabbed him around the waist and began to cry.

"Easy," he said, turning and gathering her into his arms. "I'll be back before so very long."

She looked up at him with red and swollen eyes. "That's not what I've been hearing from these people."

"Then don't listen to them," Longarm told her. "They're good, hardworking folks, but I'm a seasoned lawman and know what I'm up against in Gunshot. And don't worry, because I have no desire to die young."

Their eyes met and she studied him closely. "Does anyone ever think they're going to die before they grow old?"

"Of course. Julie, stay here and watch out over these people. I won't be around to protect you for a while and that's what worries me the most. So, if strangers appear, you need to get inside and put a gun in your hand. Trust no one."

"All right."

"Caleb and Henry will fight and so will Liam. If you're threatened, stand together and you should be all right. I just wish that I could be here to make sure."

"Hurry back as soon as you can and don't take any chances," she urged. "If you even *think* that someone suspects you are a lawman, then leave on the run. Billy Vail and the rest of them can contact the army at Fort Cannon and let them handle the trouble."

"I'll do that."

"Promise?"

"Yes, I promise."

Julie finally let him go. And because Longarm hated sad farewells, he mounted his buckskin and rode off at a gallop, not looking back until he had ridden almost a mile. Even so, Julie was still standing where he'd left her, and the little cabin, corrals, fields, and outbuildings sure did look small and vulnerable.

Longarm waved and the woman from Denver waved back. Then, he reined the horse back to the north and rode on, wondering what new and dangerous challenges this day would bring. His hands stung from the busted blisters and his back ached from all the hard-rock digging they'd done last night.

He returned to the valley where he'd shot the four killers and rapists. Vultures had gathered to feast. Longarm's expression hardened as he rode past the mass of fighting, squawking birds. He didn't look to see how fast they were consuming the four outlaws, but from the number of birds, he felt sure that the bodies wouldn't be intact long enough to rot in this heat. What the vultures didn't eat today the coyotes and other scavengers would certainly finish tonight.

His horse was tired, but Longarm pushed it through that valley of death and on many more miles before the sun went down. He located a small spring up in the rocks and hobbled the weary gelding so that it could nourish itself on the spring-fed grass. Then, he chose a resting place up in some rocks, where he had a commanding view of the land, and he quickly made a cold supper of bread, cheese, and apples.

That night he suffered from bad dreams filled with revolting, hungry, red-necked vultures. He awoke well before daylight and built a fire to make cowboy coffee and to smoke a cigar until the sun peeked over the eastern horizon. It was warm already, and he knew the day would soon be hot.

How far was he from Gunshot? Would there be armed

guards in the hills leading to its approach? Longarm had
no idea. He'd ridden into outlaw strongholds before and
had found them to be surprisingly vulnerable, often with
no guards present. It was his theory that outlaws were, by
their very nature, overconfident, self-indulgent, and typi-
cally lazy. They tended to believe that the rest of mankind
feared them and so were generally lax in regard to their
own protection.

He saddled up and was riding again before the sun was
barely off the horizon. Longarm had talked to Caleb long
enough to get detailed directions to Gunshot, but the man
had been fairly vague about the distances. Even so, Longarm felt that he was less than thirty miles from the outlaw
stronghold.

He still had the phony wanted posters folded and
stashed in his saddlebags, but he didn't know exactly how
or where he could use them. Wouldn't do much good just
to tack them up to a pine tree in this empty country, even
if he had a nail or tack. Longarm finally decided that, if
he were stopped by the Gunshot Gang, he'd just pull out
the posters and brag about how he had a big reward on
his head. That might work, and if it failed, he'd have to
do some fast talking and thinking.

When the sun was directly overhead, Longarm headed for
a stand of big pines up near a towering red bluff. He
estimated that the temperature was very close to one hundred degrees even though he had been climbing steadily.
That meant that it was even hotter back down at Lee's
Ferry, and he hoped that Julie and the women were stay-
ing inside, where it was cool and comfortable. He tried
not to think of what would become of Mrs. Evans, who
was no longer young and pretty. But Henry would take
care of his mother because he was a fine young man; it
gave Longarm no small amount of satisfaction to think
that he'd played a crucial role in Henry's survival.

The other widow, Mrs. Huddle, was quite a bit younger

and still somewhat attractive. She'd grieve for a while, and soon the eligible bachelors for miles around would come calling. If the woman was resilient and able to get past the loss of her husband, she'd be able to pick and choose among many suitors because western men vastly outnumbered the available women.

Longarm gave the buckskin free rein and allowed the animal to pick its own way up through the talus slope and into the pines. When they came to a stop in the blessed shade, he looked around for signs of water but saw none. The horse was thirsty so that meant that they would not long remain up in this shaded place.

He unsaddled the buckskin to dry out its back, then used his saddle as a pillow. Flies buzzed overheard, but he covered his face with his hat and soon dozed off.

Several hours later, Longarm was awakened by the soft nickering coupled with the stamping feet of his tall gelding. Longarm's hand went to the gun at his side without thinking and he sat up, fully alert. At first, he saw nothing. But then, he wisely followed the gaze of his horse and that was when he saw the horseman. The man was slumped over in his saddle, obviously asleep or badly hurt. A second horse was following, and it carried another man, only this one was either dead or unconscious because he was draped over his saddle and tied down to keep him from falling.

Longarm stood up and backed his horse deeper into the pines. Who were these men and what was the nature of their business? As the horseman came nearer, Longarm made the decision that the upright man was badly wounded and struggling to stay in his saddle. And because he was headed straight for Gunshot, the odds were that he was an outlaw and most likely one who had been shot while trying to commit some crime against man or his property.

What should I do? Go down and offer to help? Sure, why not?

77

Because the wounded outlaw was moving so slowly, Longarm was in no hurry. He wiped the buckskin's back with a towel, making sure that it was dry and that there were no burrs or stickers before he saddled the animal. Then he tightened his cinch and mounted. He rode at an oblique angle toward the outlaw so that he would have every advantage.

"Hello up there!" he called when the outlaw's horse twisted its neck around and whinnied a greeting.

The wounded rider must have been dozing in his saddle because Longarm's words startled him quite badly. His head snapped up and he fumbled for the six-gun at his side.

Longarm shouted, drawing his own weapon. "I mean you no harm. In fact, I might even be able to help."

The outlaw's hand still gripped his gun, but when he tried to drag it out of his holster, it was clear that the movement require a supreme effort. Seeing that Longarm had the drop on him, the outlaw relaxed and placed his hands on his saddle horn.

"Don't shoot," he said wearily. "I give up."

Longarm pushed the buckskin forward, and when he passed the man draped over his horse, he saw that he had been shot twice in the back. He'd died on the run. And the survivor was also shot twice, but both wounds were high in his right shoulder. The back of the man's shirt was caked black with dried blood and Longarm could see that his face was very pale.

"I'm heading for Gunshot," Longarm said. "If you're going to the same town, maybe I can help you."

"Don't need no help," the wounded man muttered. "You the law or what?"

"I'm on the run," Longarm explained. "Maybe like you."

The man looked terrible. His eyes were sunken in his long, angular face and his skin was the flat, lifeless, gray color of a grave stone. At first glance, Longarm thought

78

him to be in his fifties. But at closer inspection, he revised that estimate down to the mid-thirties.

"What's your name?" the outlaw asked.

"Custis Long." Longarm knew the name would mean nothing, and he saw no reason to make this any more complicated than necessary. "I've got a bounty on my head and I heard that a man can hide out for a spell in Gunshot."

"Some men can."

"You're shot up pretty bad," Longarm said, noting that the man's saddlebags were bulging. "I think we need to get you on the ground and have a look at those wounds."

The man stared at him, breathing in hard, shallow gulps. Finally, he whispered, "You a doctor or something?"

"No, but—"

"Then leave me alone," the man hissed, cold sweat beading his forehead.

"Are you also on the way to Gunshot?"

He stared at Longarm in suspicious silence. "You ask a lot of questions for a man on the run. Maybe you . . ."

The rider leaned sideways, gave a sharp gasp, and tumbled out of his saddle. When he hit the ground like a millstone, Longarm heard all the breath burst from his lungs. Longarm dismounted and knelt beside the fallen man and rolled him over to stare at his face. He reached for his pulse and it was weak and racing.

"Can you hear me?"

The outlaw's eyes fluttered open. He stared up at Longarm, but was unable to focus.

"What's your name?"

"Dean," the man gasped, fighting hard to regain his breath. "Dean Hall. My dead friend is Dub Beason."

"What happened?"

"We robbed a Colorado bank and they shot us up as we rode out. Tell—" Dean shuddered, grabbing Longarm by the wrist and squeezing until the tendons stood out in

79

his neck. Longarm thought he was dying right then, but the outlaw quivered and his eyes bulged with an effort to stay conscious. "Tell my brother to wipe out the town of . . ."

Suddenly, the heels of the man's boots began to pound the dirt and Longarm heard the familiar death rattle in the outlaw's throat. He knew that Hall was a goner even before the man expelled his final breath.

Longarm searched Hall's pockets but found only a few dollars, a barlow knife, and a few silver coins. Nothing else except a pretty good pocket watch. He walked over to Dub Beason. The man was stiff and there was nothing interesting or of value in any of his pockets. But when Longarm unbuckled the saddlebags on both horses, he found grain sacks stuffed with greenbacks.

"Holy cow," he whispered, extracting the bags and then dumping all the cash on top of a nearby flat rock. Quickly counting the money, it totaled up to almost three thousand dollars. "Wonder which Colorado bank they hit."

There were no papers with the money and no way of knowing where it had come from. But that would not be difficult to determine. Three thousand dollars was quite a haul in this country and, had he been near a telegraph office, Longarm felt certain that he could have soon discovered the origin of the bank money.

He stuffed the cash back into the sacks and leaned against the rock. What he had here was an important decision to make. If Longarm delivered the stolen money to Gunshot, he would be judged either a Good Samaritan or a fool. Certainly not a wanted man. On the other hand, if he did not show up in Gunshot with the cash, the outlaws would probably learn about the holdup anyway and then realize he'd held out on them.

"Well," Longarm said, looking at the two dead men. "You've kind of put me in a fix. I'm damned if I play it straight with the Gunshot Gang and damned if I don't!"

He lit a half-smoked cigar and considered his predicament carefully. What he must do, Longarm decided, was to react to this windfall exactly like an outlaw . . . a wanted man.

"I'll turn in one thousand dollars and hide the rest," he muttered to himself. "And if they find out that I've held out on them in Gunshot, well, that's exactly what a rough character on the run would do."

His decision made, Longarm wasted no time in dividing the money into a small package to hand over to the men at Gunshot when he delivered the bodies, and the other two thousand he would hide under some rocks for safe-keeping.

Thirty minutes later, he had Dean Hall lashed across his saddle just like Dub Beason. Then, taking up the reins to their horses, he mounted his own buckskin and headed down the trail to Gunshot, wondering what kind of a re-ception he'd receive.

Longarm sure hoped that bringing this pair in would disarm the Gunshot Gang of any suspicions. They'd of course want to know the circumstances surrounding how he'd found this dead pair, and he'd tell them the truth. Then he'd let them search him and find the thousand dollars he'd placed in his own saddlebags. They'd demand to know if there was more bank money and he'd lie and tell them that there was not. They might even rough him up a little to make sure that he hadn't held out on them. But Longarm knew that he could handle rough treatment. The main thing was that they believed he was a liar and a cheat with a bounty on his head. That he was, in short, just as low-down and dishonest as were they.

"Come on," Longarm said to his horse as he led the other two animals along behind. "I'm hot, tired, and hun-gry. Maybe they have food in Gunshot and some whiskey. Maybe," he said with a wry smile, "they even have a few pretty women to keep the boys company."

And so, as he rode along, Longarm considered how in one damned hot day, the gang had lost six of its members.

Four that he'd killed and the two that the people of some as-yet-unknown Colorado town had killed.

Six down, and he wondered how many yet to go before all the rattlesnakes in Gunshot were eliminated.

Chapter 8

Longarm rode all that day, moving west, higher onto the Kaibab Plateau, Arizona's pine covered North Rim country. He had passed all the landmarks that Caleb had described and knew that he was close to Gunshot, but he wasn't exactly sure how close. And so, as darkness fell over the high rim country, he made another cold camp, but not before he'd lifted the stiff bodies of Dean Hall and Dub Beason from their mounts and laid them out side by side next to his campfire. It was a little eerie to sleep beside two dead men, but Longarm wasn't squeamish and he spent a restful night in the pines.

The next morning, he awoke just after dawn, made coffee, and finished the last of the food that he'd been given by the Mormons down at Lee's Ferry. He resaddled the horses, then carried the stiff bodies of Dean and Dub over to their horses one by one. The animals didn't want anything to do with their former owners and shied away, eyeballs rolling at the sight and scent of death. But when they reached the end of their tethers, Longarm was able to pitch the two dead outlaws across their saddles and lash them down tightly.

"Don't worry," he said, stroking the necks of the nervous horses. "You shouldn't have to carry these bodies very far."

Longarm remounted, then moved out with a thousand dollars of cash stuffed into his saddlebags. He knew that he would soon catch sight of Gunshot, and he hoped that he would not receive an unpleasant welcome when he arrived.

At about ten o'clock in the morning, he topped a low butte and saw the outlaw stronghold. From a distance of two miles, it appeared to be like any other small frontier settlement, only it was a bit more run-down. There was a main street lined with business establishments, a couple of larger structures that were probably either hay barns, saloons or liveries and a creek that meandered just to the north.

If I didn't know better, I'd think it was just a little Mormon ranching community, he thought as he pushed his buckskin into a trot.

As he neared Gunshot, he saw two men approaching him on foot, and they were armed with rifles.

"Must be the town's welcoming committee," he said to his horse.

Longarm raised his left hand and waved in greeting, but the pair didn't show any signs of being friendly. Instead, they lifted their rifles to their chests, planted their feet wide apart, and waited for him to come closer.

"Mornin'," he called, drawing his horse up when he was still about twenty yards distant. "I have some bodies and some cash to deliver to whoever is running the show in Gunshot."

"Who are you?" the taller of the pair demanded. "And whose bodies are they?"

"Dean Hall and Dub Beason," he replied. "They robbed a Colorado bank but got shot all to pieces. When I met them yesterday, Dub was already finished and Dean died soon after we met. His dying wish was that his body be delivered to his brother."

84

The two sentries exchanged solemn glances. Finally, the taller one said, "Lift your hands up over your head, mister."

"Hellfire," Longarm complained, "do you think I'd ride in here if I wanted any trouble with you jaspers? I'm doing your dead friends a big favor and—"

"Shut up!" the shorter of the pair ordered as he and his friend moved forward. The short one kept an eye on Longarm while the taller one inspected the bodies.

"It's Dean and Dub all right. Both of 'em were shot in the back."

"That's right," Longarm said. "Dean Hall said that they rode out of the town in a hail of bullets. I guess their holdup didn't go as well as they'd planned."

"Who are you?"

"Custis Long."

"Well maybe you shot Dean and Dub."

"Then why would I bring them here?" Longarm gave the man a look of pure disgust. "That would be pretty stupid, wouldn't it?"

"You look stupid," the tall man snapped. "What is your business in this part of the country?"

"I need a place to hole up for a while, where I won't be bothered by the law. I heard about Gunshot and figured this was the safest place for a wanted man to hide. Then, when I came across those two men, I tried to help them out but I was too late to do 'em much good."

The tall one came over and tore open Longarm's saddlebags. He stared at the cash, then used his knife to cut the saddlebags free. Hoisting them up, he smiled and said, "Trace is going to be pretty unhappy about his brother dyin', but he'll sure be glad to see all this cash."

"He's going to be more than unhappy," the shorter man commented. "He's going to go crazy. Nobody will want to be near him for a few days."

"Mind if I lower my hands?" Longarm asked. "They're getting kind of heavy."

The taller man reached up and removed Longarm's pistol from its holster. "All right, lower 'em," he growled.

Longarm placed his hands on his saddle horn. "I thought maybe I'd at least get a 'thanks' for bringing in the cash your friends died stealing," he said in a peevish voice. "And I'd like some of it as sort of a reward for doing you boys a favor."

"Oh," the tall man said, "you can be sure that you'll be rewarded, all right!" He winked to his sidekick. "Ain't that right, Jess?"

"Sure is," Jess replied. He turned to his friend. "Do you think that Trace is awake yet?"

"Probably not. He was with that new woman all night, and I heard them scratchin' and clawin' each other all night."

"Lucky bastard," Jess groused. "How come Trace always gets first pick of the women?"

"Why don't you ask him and find out?"

"No thanks," Jess said. "You're going to hand Trace that pair of saddlebags, ain't you?"

"Sure." The tall man looked up at Longarm. "Climb down from that buckskin horse and start walking toward town, leading them other two animals."

"I ain't much for walking when I can ride," Longarm snapped.

"Do what I say or I'll shoot you in both knees, and then you'll never walk again anyway."

Longarm dismounted and started walking toward Gunshot, knowing that the two men had their rifles trained on his back. He walked right into town noting that it looked exactly like any other ranching community except that there were two gunsmithing shops instead of the one that would normally serve a small town.

His arrival with the bodies of two of the gang's members caused quite a stir. Rough-looking men poured out of the businesses and saloons to stare at the procession, and no one was offering Longarm any thanks.

"Hold up," Jess ordered when they stopped before a nameless building, which looked as if it would topple in a high wind. "I'll go inside and tell Trace that his brother is dead."

Longarm said nothing as he tied his buckskin to a hitching rail, then loosened its cinch. That accomplished, he reached into his pocket and found a cigar, which he lit while staring back at maybe twenty hard-faced outlaws who were glaring at him as if he were infected with the plague.

A moment later, he heard a man roar in anger, then the sound of his boots as he stomped across a wooden floor to burst outside.

"Where is he!"

"He's on the dun horse, Trace. You'll see that he was shot twice in the back."

Trace was an athletic-appearing man of ordinary size who moved like a cat . . . fast and fluid. He was clearly the best-dressed man in Gunshot and wore black pants, a black hat, and a white silk shirt that was long overdue for a good washing and ironing. He also wore a red bandana around his neck and a pearl-handled Colt on his lean hip. He would have been considered a very handsome man except for a terrible, ragged scar that ran from his mouth to his right eye, twisting both and giving the man an odd, evil expression. Longarm judged him to be in his mid-twenties, beardless but with a handlebar mustache twisted and waxed at the tips.

Trace grabbed his brother's head and tipped it up. It was a pretty hideous sight, being bloated with blood. Longarm watched the man's expression to see if it registered pain or sadness, but all he saw was anger and hatred.

"Who did this!" he demanded, directing a pair of smoldering brown eyes up at Custis.

"I don't know. He was dying when I came upon him and the other fella. He told me that you'd give me a reward if I brought his body and the bank money they managed to get away with in to Gunshot."

"Dean told you that I would give you a *reward*?" the outlaw leader asked, his voice dropping until it reminded Longarm of the whisper of a snake.

"That's right. He didn't want his body to be left for the vultures."

"If he said that then he lied," Trace said, that terrible scar seeming to turn even paler against the backdrop of his swarthy face. "And to tell you the truth, mister, I think that *you're* the liar."

"I could have left those two bodies for the buzzards and ridden off to California or Nevada. Instead, I brought you one thousand dollars of some bank's money," Longarm told the man. "I figure that ought to mean something."

"Yeah, it does," Trace agreed. "But I'm already wondering how much more money you kept for yourself."

"None," Longarm said tightly.

"We'll see."

Two women stepped out of the building and onto the porch. Both were young and attractive, especially the short, voluptuous one with the long, shiny black hair and smoldering black eyes. She wasn't pure Mexican or Indian, but Longarm guessed she had some of the blood of one or both races. She wore a low-cut blouse and struck a pose, hands resting on her shapely hips. Longarm met her eyes and almost forgot about Trace Hall.

That was a mistake because Trace's gun appeared in his hand almost as if by magic, and he pointed it at Longarm, cocking back the hammer and saying, "Don't you dare even think about that woman."

"Sorry. But a man can't help but admire beauty." He said that loud enough for the woman to hear his words and that brought a smile to her mouth.

Trace jammed his Colt into Longarm's chest saying, "Tell me the truth. What really happened to my brother and how much money did they get from that bank?"

"I told you the truth."

"You're lying," Trace snarled. "I can always tell when a man is lying to me and I can smell his fear."

"I'm *not* lying," Longarm said, heart pounding against his ribs. "I was coming here looking for a place to hide from the law. I came across your brother and that other man who was already dead. Then I brought them here with the money they stole. And dammit, I'm not too damned happy about your gun in my chest after doing you a favor!"

He'd made his voice sound angry and insulted while praying that his outrage would convince Trace that he was telling the truth.

It worked. Trace relaxed and uncocked the hammer of his gun. "What is your name?"

"Custis Long."

"Why are you running from the law?"

"I had a difference of opinion with the marshal of Laramie, Wyoming."

"And?"

"I killed him."

Trace swung around to look at tough members of his gang. "Anyone know the name of the marshal of Laramie?"

"I was there a couple years ago," a short, stocky man with legs like tree stumps said. "The bastard's name was—"

"Shut up!" Trace commanded. He turned back to Longarm. "What was the marshal's name?"

Longarm had worked with the marshal of Laramie several times, so it was a safe, easy question to answer. "His name was Ray Hooker. He was about forty. Too old and slow to be a town marshal. I outdrew him and I heard that the town gave him a real nice burial with flowers and words from the Bible."

"You killed Marshal Hooker?" the man who'd spoken up asked, looking thoroughly impressed. "Marshal Hooker was one tough bastard!"

"Yeah, but he was past his prime," Longarm answered. "I put two bullets in his chest before he even cleared leather. Because of that, there's a five hundred dollar reward on my head."

"Is that so?" Trace asked, still looking suspicious.

"It is," Longarm said, unable to keep his eyes from raking the sensual young woman who was staring at him so boldly. He regained his focus and said to Trace, "I've taken no small pleasure in collecting a few of the reward posters on myself. Seemed like a healthy thing to do when I was last up in Wyoming. You can take a look at them in my saddlebags, if you please. But I'm handsomer than the sketches."

Trace almost smiled. Maybe he did smile, but because of the scar across his lips, it looked like a twisted snarl. "Which saddlebag?"

"The one on the other side of my horse."

"Get it out and show me."

Longarm was more than happy to oblige. He carefully unfolded the wanted posters that Billy Vail had had made up in their Denver federal building just before he and Julie had departed.

Trace unfolded the wanted posters and studied the sketch, then read the text, his deformed lips moving as he struggled over the words. Finished, he looked up at Longarm as if to compare the sketch with the man and then he said, "All right. Any man with guts enough to gun down a town marshal and then ride around collecting his wanted posters is welcome here in Gunshot."

Longarm decided to push his luck. "What about a reward for bringing in the bodies of your brother and his friend?"

"Are you dead broke?"

"No. I've got some money . . . but not much."

"Then spend it here."

"I expected more," Longarm said, leaving no doubt of his dissatisfaction.

90

Trace spun around on his heel, but not before taking all the bank's cash. "Your reward is your life. You can stay until I say you have to leave, or else earn your keep like everyone else in Gunshot."

"Thanks a hell of a lot!" Longarm called as several men came over and collected the horses and bodies, then led them off, leaving him standing alone in front of the saloon.

Trace went up to the two women. He put his arm around the one who had been watching Longarm so closely and then he put his arm around the other as well. Longarm heard the voices of other women inside the building. It was the place, he reasoned, where the favored were invited for their rewards.

Then Trace and the two women disappeared into the building. The man didn't even look back at the body of his dead brother before the door closed behind him.

Longarm wasn't sure what was expected of him so he stepped forward, but a brutish looking outlaw blocked his path and growled, "Just where the hell do you think you're going?"

"Inside to see if I can get whiskey."

"You don't go in there unless Trace invites you in to talk business. Understand?"

"Then where the hell do I find a drink?" Longarm challenged. "I'm tired, out of sorts, and thirsty, so I'd advise you not to push me."

"I'll push anyone I please."

"Is that right?" Longarm asked, noticing that everyone was still watching him, to see how he would react to this threat

"That's right. And I also think you're a liar."

"What's your name?" Longarm asked in a pleasant voice.

The man blinked, then said, "Eli."

"Well, Eli, your boss might get away with calling me a liar, but you can't."

91

"Oh yeah?"

Eli stepped back and swung his big, meaty fist at Longarm's jaw. Ducking, Longarm delivered a tremendous uppercut to the man's gut, doubling him over gasping for air. When Eli fumbled for his Colt, Longarm laced his fingers together and brought both fists down like a sledgehammer across the side of the outlaw's neck.

Eli went down and Longarm knew that he wouldn't get up. Stepping over him, Longarm smiled coldly at the other outlaws. "All right, boys. Fun and games are over. Now where can I wet my whistle before someone else gets hurt?"

"Over there," a man said, pointing to a building just up the street. "Every man in Gunshot gets the first drink free. The rest cost five cents."

"Fair enough. What about my horse and saddle?"

"They ain't going anywhere. Cost you two bits a day to keep 'em here, though."

Longarm swore just loud enough for the gang to hear him and think he was angry. Then he started for the saloon muttering, "I guess Gunshot is a little shy on repaying a man for his kindnesses."

"Ain't no kindnesses wanted or needed in this town, mister," the same man told him. "Just mind your manners and try not to start any bad trouble."

"Or what happens?" Longarm demanded to know as he stopped and turned on the outlaw.

"Trace will decide your punishment. He either uses his bullwhip on you . . . or he challenges you to a gunfight. First one hurts like hell, second one kills you deader than someone killed his brother and poor Dub Beason."

Longarm glared at the man and his friends, who continued to watch him as if two heads instead of one rested on his broad shoulders. Then, he went to have a few drinks of whiskey. Not enough to dull his thinking and reactions, but enough to calm his nerves.

So far, so good, he thought as he stepped into what passed in Gunshot as a saloon.

Other men came into the bar and ordered drinks. Longarm noticed that most of them paid their nickel. Surprisingly, the whiskey hadn't been watered down and was of good quality. No doubt it had been stolen. Only the one man who had warned him outside seemed interested in having any conversation. He was pretty young to be running with this rough caliber of outlaws. Longarm doubted that he was even twenty-one, and he looked like a choirboy.

"My name is Gavin," he said in the form of an introduction. "I haven't been here but a few days myself."

"Then that would explain why you are willing to talk to me."

"Ah," Gavin said, smiling easily. "These fellas aren't so bad as long as you let them alone."

"I'll leave them alone if they'll do the same for me," Longarm said. "What are you hiding here for?"

"I killed a man," Gavin said, shaking his head. "Over a girl we both thought was true to us."

"Too bad."

"I loved my sweet Nellie very much and so did Pete. She said she'd marry me, then Nellie changed her mind and told Pete the same thing. We got into a fight over in Cripple Creek and I killed my best friend."

"How?"

"Shot him in the belly with his own gun. It was either that, or he would have shot me."

"That sounds like self-defense."

"You'd think so," Gavin said, eyes bleak. "But Pete's father was the town banker, and he wanted me hanged. I had to run, but not before I went to see Nellie. She was out at her father's mining claim, but when he saw me he opened fire with his rifle. Shot my horse out from under me and I was pinned down by the creek. He came running and I managed to drag out my Colt and I killed him dead."

"As he was trying to kill you?"

"That's right. But he was just as dead as poor Pete. Then Nellie started screaming and acting crazy. She

93

picked up the rifle, pointed it at me, and tried to shoot me dead while my leg was still pinned under my horse."

Longarm shook his head. "So what happened then?"

Gavin unbuttoned his shirt and Longarm saw a round, black scab. "Nellie drilled me right here, in the ribs. Rifle bullet went in the front and came out the back. I had no choice."

"You killed her, too?"

Tears came to the young man's eyes. "What else could I do? She was the cause of all my grief. Hadn't been for her lying to me and Pete, none of it would have happened. But first, I pleaded with her one last time to drop her rifle. She didn't. She shot my horse in the head, and I shot her in the head. Dropped like a bag of rocks into the creek and the current swept her away."

Longarm could hardly believe this tale of woe. But he only had to stare into Gavin's tortured eyes to see that every word of it was true. "So how did you get out from under the horse to escape?"

"It wasn't easy. I used the barrel of my gun to dig away the rocks and sand until I could pull free. Then, I hobbled over to the cabin and found a shovel. I buried Nellie's father and went hiking down the river until I found poor, sweet Nellie's body snagged up on the roots of a tree. I almost shot myself I was so crazed with grief. But I didn't, so I buried her in the mud, then went back to the mining claim and found where her old man had hidden his gold. I took it knowing that I'd need it to save my life."

"Did you give it all to Trace in exchange for him allowing you to stay here?"

"Yeah," Gavin said quietly.

Longarm saw the lie in the lad's eyes and knew that Gavin had, just like himself, held most of the money back for himself.

At least he's got that much sense, Longarm thought as the bartender brought them both another glass of whiskey.

Chapter 9

Longarm had a couple of drinks, then wandered outside and sat down in a rickety old chair that faced the street. Gunshot didn't have a boardwalk or any porches, but the chair was in the shade and, since he had no idea what he was to do or what was expected of him, he figured he might as well relax and watch the town's limited activity.

There wasn't much to watch, really. A few riders came and went, and Longarm counted three saloons along with the usual shops. The difference between Gunshot and a normal town was that he didn't see any women or children. Just men, and most of them looked as if they'd slit a man's throat for a nickel.

Longarm tipped the flat brim of his hat down low over his eyes, but not so low that he couldn't see things. He also used an empty chair beside him as a footstool. The arrangement proved so comfortable that he fell asleep after a while and didn't awaken until a voice asked, "Hey, are you gettin' hungry?"

Longarm snapped awake and tipped the brim of his snuff-colored hat back. He looked up to see Trace Hall watching him closely.

"As a matter of fact I am," Longarm, said, realizing

that the sun was almost ready to set on the horizon. "I haven't eaten a good meal for weeks."

"Well, you're about to have one now," Trace said, looking friendlier than he had earlier. "Come on, and let's have a steak and some whiskey. I like to get to know the kind of men who visit Gunshot. Sometimes I let them stay and sometimes I don't. But everyone has to bring in their little contribution. You brought yours, but that doesn't mean you can stay as long as you wish."

"If you don't want me here," Longarm told the man, "just say so and I'll be on my way. I was thinking that I might like to see California."

Trace stopped and turned. He was about four inches shorter than Longarm and some thirty pounds lighter, but he somehow seemed bigger than his actual size. The man had a fixed gaze and a commanding presence that could not be ignored. Longarm had the strong impression that he was arrogant and fearless.

"California is overrated. Are you any good with that gun on your hip?" Trace asked.

"I've seen worse."

Trace reached up with a forefinger and stroked the waxed tip of his mustache. Then he looked around and spotted a big mongrel ambling down the street. "You told me that your name was Custis Long, didn't you?"

"That's right."

"Well, Custis, why don't you show me how fast you can draw iron and shoot that dog."

Longarm studied the dog. "I like animals," he said. "And they like me. Why don't we let him go about his own business?"

"Why?" Trace asked. "Because I don't like that particular dog. You see that big banner of a tail he waves?"

"Yep."

"I'm going to shoot it off. Want to bet me five dollars I can't?"

Longarm curbed his outrage, knowing that a man

96

wanted for murder would never make the fate of a dog into a life or death issue. "I'd rather you let him keep his tail."

Trace laughed, drew his gun and fired as fast as anyone Longarm had ever seen. Only instead of blowing off the mongrel's tail, he shot the poor animal in the belly. The poor, unsuspecting mongrel howled and began to thrash about on the ground.

"You should have bet me," Trace said, starting to walk away.

Longarm clenched his teeth in anger and it took every ounce of his willpower not to knock Trace Hall down and stomp him to a pulp. He detested men who hurt women and animals for no reason other than their own orneriness.

"Hey!" he shouted at the departing outlaw leader. "Aren't you at least going to put the poor son-of-a-bitch out of its misery?"

"The world is full of misery," Trace replied with a shrug of his shoulders. "I would have thought that the man who gunned down a town marshal would understand that."

"Killing without reason or purpose is stupid and senseless," Longarm said recklessly.

"I had a purpose," Trace said, eyes narrowing. "I wanted to see your reaction."

"And?"

"I don't know," the man said with a cruel smile as his gaze flicked between Longarm and the dying dog. "But I'm thinking that, if you can't stand to watch a mere mongrel die, perhaps you really don't belong in Gunshot."

"You killed him on purpose, didn't you."

Trace studied the howling dog for a moment, then he nodded. "That's something I want you to wonder about. Did I shoot him in the gut by intention . . . or mistake?"

Longarm didn't care. He couldn't stand to see the dog suffer, so he drew his six-gun, took careful aim, and put the poor suffering beast out of its misery with a bullet to its dying brain.

"All right," Trace said, "you're accurate, but that didn't show me if you are fast on the draw or not."

"Yeah," Longarm said, mad clear through. "I wanted you to wonder about that."

Trace understood and laughed. Then he turned on his heel and led Longarm into the same building where he'd gone before with the two women.

"This one is mine," Trace said, slipping his arm around the dark-haired and dark-eyed woman that had watched Longarm with such bold curiosity. "Her name is Noleta."

"Interesting name," Longarm said. "What does it mean?"

"It is Latin," she told him in a voice that held an unfamiliar accent. "Where I was born, it means 'little olive.'"

"And where was that?"

"Greece," she said proudly. "And where are you from?"

"Nowhere and everywhere."

Trace bent and kissed the soft protruding mounds of Noleta's breasts, then sighed theatrically. "Like I told you, this woman is mine and only mine. If anyone comes sniffing around Noleta . . . I'll kill them. Understood?"

"Sure." Longarm turned his attention to the other woman, who was also plenty easy on the eyes. "And what is your name?"

"Rosa," she said. "I am part Mexican, part Irish. A mongrel much like everyone else other than Noleta."

"You are also very beautiful."

Rosa dipped her chin and smiled. "Thank you. I hear that often, but not usually from such a big, handsome hombre as yourself."

Trace, unable to stand someone else receiving either compliments or attention, snapped, "Why don't we cut the crap and I'll show you the other women."

Longarm was then led into a large room that was surprisingly well decorated with hand-carved furniture, paintings, rugs, and even a couple of crystal chandeliers. There was a partial second floor fronted by a balcony. He could see men and women coming and going from a line of small upstairs rooms and knew this was where Trace's favorite men were being serviced by the women.

"This is where I entertain my friends," Trace announced with a sweep of his hand that included everyone and everything. "Custis, if you want to return, you're going to have to prove to me that you deserve my friendship . . . and that of these lovely women."

Longarm understood. This was where the rewards were given out to the men of the Gunshot Gang. If you were in favor and did well, you were invited to dine and drink and then indulge yourself with these hard but desirable women.

"Martha, Billy, Ellen, Janice, Belle, this rough-looking fella is Custis Long. If we are to believe him and the wanted poster we found in his saddlebag, he killed the marshal in Laramie. And he brought in my brother . . . the crazy bastard . . . as well as Dub Beason, who we all know was as dumb as a post."

The women laughed, except for Noleta and Rosa. Out of the corner of his eye, Longarm saw both women stiffen and pale ever so slightly, and it made him wonder if they had loved either or both of the two dead outlaws that he'd packed into town.

"All right then!" Trace shouted. "Where in blazes is my piano player!"

A thin, unwell-looking man in his sixties jumped out of a side room as if he were attached to Trace by some invisible noose around his scrawny neck. He smiled and shuffled over to a battered piano by the west wall of the big dining room and saloon. Almost instantly there was music, and it was far better than most saloons could have boasted of from a battered old piano. The man played so well, in fact, that Longarm was sure that he was one of those individuals found in the West who had, at some point in their earlier eastern life, received formal musical training.

"Old Abraham tells me he was once an aspiring classical pianist back East among the hoity-toity crowd. He says that he came from a well-respected family, the son of a senator from Illinois, for gawd sakes! Can you believe that when you look at him now?"

Trace guffawed and slapped his thigh. He signaled for a round of drinks and they were brought almost instantly by a sweating Indian woman who was missing all her teeth.

"Drink up and get acquainted with the ladies!" Trace ordered. "This is your well-deserved reward for bringing in two of my men and a thousand dollars cash! It was an excellent first contribution."

"Thanks a lot," Longarm said without any sincerity. Trace dragged Noleta away to leave him standing beside Rosa, who said, "Would you like to dance?"

"I'm not much for dancing," Longarm replied, sipping his whiskey. "Why don't we mosey on over to that couch and sit and talk."

"And what would someone like you and someone like myself have to talk about?"

"I have no idea. But if we can't think of anything, then we might want to find us a bed upstairs."

"Not if you just get drunk."

"I won't get drunk," Longarm promised as he led the handsome young woman over to the couch. When they were seated, he asked. "How did someone like you wind up in a hellhole like this?"

She blinked with surprise, then gave him the faintest of a smile. "If you say that in front of Trace, he would be offended."

"And that would be bad?"

"Worse than bad . . . maybe fatal. He has killed many men. He would not think twice about killing you as well."

100

"I'll try and remember that," Longarm told her. "But listen, I've lived with two dead men for the last twenty-four hours. I'd kind of like to put the idea of dying behind me for at least a few hours. Can't we talk about something pleasant?"

"What do you have in mind?" Rosa asked. "There is little of the good to talk about in Gunshot. It is a town with no soul and no mercy."

"So why are you here?"

"I was brought here by a man I thought I loved," she said, avoiding his eyes. "I didn't know what kind of a town this was until it was too late and there was no escape for me."

"What happened to the man you loved?"

"*Thought* I loved," she corrected. "He was shot to death by Trace, but only after he beat me very badly." She turned her face away so that it was exposed to the most light. "Do you see that the shape of my nose is ruined?"

"Yes, but you're still pretty."

"And do the see the faint scar under my cheekbone?" she asked, ignoring his compliment.

"Hardly visible."

Rosa turned back to face him. "When I came here, I was no virgin. I would never try to get your sympathy by saying I was . . . how do you put it . . . pure as the driven snow. Uh-uh. I was well used and should have known better than to fall in love with such a bad man."

"You're not the first to be fooled, and you won't be the last." Longarm sipped his whiskey. "But that doesn't explain why you stay."

"I stay," Rosa said in a barely audible voice, "because I would be killed if I tried to escape."

"I see."

"But someday, Trace and all these men will die. And then, if Noleta and I are still alive—along with some of the other women who share our feelings about Gunshot— we will leave and never return."

"And will you leave with nothing but bad memories, a broken nose, and your scars?"

"We might also have some gold and money. Trace is a very wealthy man."

"If he's so wealthy, why doesn't he leave?"

"The answer is simple: He loves power and is consumed by his own greed," she said. "A wealthy man always wants more. So Trace sends his men out to rob, murder, and take by any and all means what is most precious and dear to others. They return, and he makes sure they are protected until their 'contribution,' as he calls it, is spent."

"I see." Longarm frowned. "I gave him his brother and a thousand dollars. I'd guess that's a pretty hefty contribution."

"You'd guess wrong. Trace felt nothing but contempt for his younger brother and the same can be said for Dub Beason, although both men were far better than himself."

"In what sense?"

Rosa considered the question for a moment, then answered. "They were not so cruel. I saw what Trace just did to that poor dog in the street. Do you know why he shot that particular dog?"

"He wanted to judge my reaction."

"Yes, but also because that dog was the strongest of all the mongrels. The one that took the bitches that he wanted. Trace was jealous of his courage and power."

"Jealous of a dog?"

"Jealous because he is *also* a dog," Rosa hissed, her voice corrupted by hatred. "And that should tell you everything you need to know about the man."

"Aren't you afraid that I'll tell Trace how you feel about him?"

"He knows," Rosa replied, voice dripping with venom. "He used me and then threw me aside for Noleta. And when he finds someone even prettier, he will do the same again."

"It sounds to me like you are in a bad fix."

"I was born in a 'bad fix.' " Rosa drank, quickly emptying her glass. "How hungry are you?"

"I can wait awhile."

"Then let's go upstairs and get it over with."

"Whoa!" he said, then lowered his voice. "Listen. You're a handsome young woman, but I never had to take one by force or because some other man ordered her to go to bed with me."

Rosa smiled without humor. "Are you going to tell me in the next breath that I *don't* have to go to bed with you?"

"That's right."

Rosa didn't believe him. He could see that much in her face before she said, "You want Noleta?"

"I find you both attractive."

"But her more than me."

"Yes," he admitted.

Rosa shrugged with indifference. "At least you are honest. She is prettier than me."

"Let's have another drink and then get out of here," Longarm suggested.

"Okay."

He got them both a fresh glass of whiskey, then Rosa led Longarm up the stairs to a room. Longarm glanced back to see that many eyes were watching them. He wondered if he could trust Rosa and decided that he ought to be careful what he said for a while. She might be a very accomplished liar.

"In here," she said, opening a door and stepping inside. There was a strong dead bolt on her door and she locked it carefully, saying, "This is where I entertain men who make important contributions to Trace and the gang."

Longarm studied the little five-by-ten-foot room. There was a bed and not much else but a nightstand, porcelain washbasin, pitcher of water, and a few dirty towels.

Rosa started to undress, but Longarm held up his hand. "This isn't necessary."

"Yes it is," she told him, eyes suddenly dull and dead.

"Look," he said, handing her one of the glasses of whiskey he had in his hand. "Why don't we just sit and talk? Maybe even tell a few jokes and have a few laughs."

"You cannot be serious."

"I am completely serious. I only make love to women who *want* to make love with me. Otherwise, it just sort of takes the fun out of it . . . if you follow my meaning."

"What has fun got to do with it?" she asked, obviously puzzled.

"Never mind. But don't undress. Just . . . just sit on your bed and tell me what you feel like talking about."

"To you, nothing." Her red lips formed a pout, and she folded her arms across her breasts and eyed him suspiciously.

"Then let's drink in silence and maybe even lie down and have a little nap before we go back down there and eat."

"I don't understand you, Custis Long. What kind of a man would—"

"Drop it," he said. "Rosa, I'm just not in the mood to play the game that Trace has set up for us. Understand?"

"No . . . but that's all right."

Longarm sipped his whiskey. It was warm upstairs; actually, it was hot. That and the liquor made him sleepy again. He stretched out on the bed and gazed with heavy eyelids up at the puzzled young woman. "I think I'll take a little siesta. Wake me up when you think that enough time has passed so that Trace will think you've fulfilled your duty."

"I will."

"Good," he said, closing his eyes and instantly dropping off to sleep.

Rosa was sleeping, too, when they were awakened by a hard pounding on their door. "Hey you two in there! Don't keep screwin' all night! It's time to eat!"

"We'll be right down, Trace," Rosa called, somehow making her voice sound a little breathless. "He . . . he is very good!"

"Ha! But I'm still the best, ain't I, you fiery little chili pepper!"

"Yes, Trace." Rosa's voice was sweet and compliant, but her eyes burned. "You are still the best."

"And I'm about ready to remind you of it again. Custis, get dressed and come on down. We got to get acquainted."

"Sure thing."

When the man stomped off, Longarm sat up and knuckled the sleep out of his eyes. "Well, it was nice napping with you, Rosa."

"Anytime. You know something?"

"What?"

"You're the first man I've ever known that had me on a bed and didn't force himself between my legs."

"Maybe I should apologize."

"No," she said. "It is I that should apologize for judging you to be like the ones below. You *are* different."

"No I'm not," he replied, unwilling to allow her to think of him in a good way and perhaps jeopardize his cover. "I'm a killer. A wanted man. I'm damn sure no saint."

She reached out and took his hand. "You are different. I want to talk to you again."

He decided to tease. "You mean you want to get a nap together?"

For the first time, Rosa really laughed. "No, I want to get to know you."

"I'm just not all that interesting or worth knowing."

"I don't believe you. I think . . ." she put her forefinger to her lips. "I think that you are not at all what you seem, Custis Long."

Longarm shook his head. "You already admitted that

you are a poor judge of men. Otherwise, you wouldn't be a prisoner in this godforsaken town."

"Yes, I have made mistakes of judgment. But not with you."

"We'd better go down," Longarm suggested. "We've been summoned by the royal highness of Gunshot and it's not an invitation to be ignored."

"Yes," she said, the warmth fading from her eyes. "Let's go down together. You must act as if we did it all the time we were alone."

"Did what?" he asked, feigning ignorance.

Rosa giggled. "Custis, if you are not killed soon, I believe I am going to like you very much."

"That could be a big if," he said, taking her hand and then leaning forward and kissing her cheek.

A tear formed in Rosa's dark eyes, then she angrily wiped it away and led him back down to where Trace was holding court.

Chapter 10

"So!" Trace bellowed, shoving Noleta off his lap and staggering to his feet. "How was she in bed?"

Everyone but Noleta and Longarm bellowed with laughter as Rosa's cheeks darkened with embarrassment. Noting it, Trace cackled, "Custis, you ought to thank me for breaking her in right! Before I taught her how to hump, she wasn't anything to remember."

Longarm felt Rosa's acute embarrassment, and it was all that he could do to form a cold smile. "She's real special, that's for sure."

"Yeah she is," Trace grudgingly agreed. "I might have to give her a try myself one of these days . . . just for old time's sake, huh, Noleta?"

Noleta said nothing.

"Aw, come on," Trace said, his plea a cold mockery. He turned to Longarm. "Custis, a man cannot live off women alone. Sit down beside me and let's eat."

Longarm was hungry, and he followed the outlaw leader over to a huge table surrounded by chairs and covered with slabs of beef. He sat down beside Trace, noting that the man was sober enough to keep Noleta on his other side.

"So," Trace began, "why don't you tell me exactly what

happened when you found my brother dying."

"All right." Longarm quickly ran through the story again, this time with a few more details. He ended by saying, "You brother died asking me to tell you good-bye."

"Well, you did and, for that, I'm grateful. Dean wasn't much of a kid brother. I knew that he'd get his ass shot to pieces the first time he went out without me to pull his fat out of the fire."

"You knew that your own brother was going to get himself killed?"

"Sure!" Trace stabbed a piece of beef off a serving plate with a long, sharp, knife. "It was just a matter of time. The thing is that I was always afraid he'd get me killed with him! Now, I don't have to worry about that any-more."

Longarm shook his head. "So much for brotherly love, huh?"

"Piss on brotherly love. My kid brother was a fool," Trace said contemptuously. "I been wipin' his nose since we were just knee high to a toadstool. I can't tell you how many times I had to bail him out of one bad fight after another. And when we was kids, I fought the big bullies off him because everyone knew he was weak. That's why I grew up so strong and tough."

"I see."

Trace jammed beef in his maw and asked, "So how tough are you, big man?"

"I can hold my own."

"Yeah, I heard about you dropping Eli. That was im-pressive. But Eli is just a big oaf. What do you think about a *real* challenge?"

"What's that supposed to mean?"

Trace winked and chewed hard. "Maybe you'd like to fight me."

Longarm didn't want to fight Trace. When he whipped the man, he'd be signing his own death warrant. And the idea of letting Trace whip him was totally repellent.

"I don't care to fight you because we'd both end up in pretty bad shape and then how would Rosa and Noleta feel about it when we couldn't service them like they deserve?"

Trace blinked and then a slow smile formed on his lips as he swallowed a mouthful of meat. "You know something, Custis? You're right. We're both too handsome to get all messed up in a stupid fight."

"I agree."

Trace slapped him on the back hard enough to rock Longarm forward in his chair, then said, "I think you and me are gonna get along pretty well. That is, as soon as you tell me where you went and hid the rest of the bank robbery money."

Longarm felt a knot form in the pit of his gut. "I told you, Trace, I gave it all to you."

"Are you dead certain about that, Custis? Make sure before you answer because I've already sent a man out to find out which bank my fool brother and his friend robbed. And I'm sure that he'll also find out how much money was taken." Trace winked. "And if the amount that the bank says was taken *don't* tally up to the same amount you handed over . . . well, I'd say that meant you lied and cheated me. And that, furthermore, you have no respect for the right to come into Gunshot and be safe from the law. A safety that we risk our lives to preserve here against any and all forms of law or government."

Longarm could feel sweat suddenly begin to drip from his armpits. He knew that this man wasn't bluffing. Knew also that someone from Gunshot would find out how much money had really been stolen. Then, he'd be trapped in the lie and Trace would probably have him strung up by the thumbs and peeled like an onion with his bullwhip. It was not something that Longarm wanted to experience.

"All right," he said, trying to form a weak smile. "Maybe I did take some of the bank loot for myself."

"Ahh-ha!" Trace cried triumphantly, surveying his grinning audience. "So now we're at the moment of truth! Exactly how much of the bank's stolen cash did you hold back for yourself, Mr. Custis Long?"

"What the hell. I held back . . . two thousand."

Trace's jaw dropped and everyone in the room gaped at the enormity of the difference between what Longarm had turned over to the gang and what he had kept for himself.

"Two thousand dollars!" Trace swore, face red with outrage.

Longarm knew he was in a terrible fix. If Trace drew his gun to shoot him, he'd kill the outlaw leader, but the others would gun him down. There was no way out of this except to act bold.

"I like expensive things," he said with a wink.

Trace had a glass of whiskey in his fist. He threw its contents into Longarm's eyes, then hit him in the belly with an uppercut. Longarm staggered backward, hand stabbing for his gun. But men grabbed and pinned his arms to his sides. He struggled for a moment, eyes burning from the whiskey.

"I'm going to teach you a lesson you won't soon forget!" Trace shouted. "Noleta, get my bullwhip! Tie that lying bastard to the column over there and strip his shirt off!"

"No!" Rosa screamed. "He was just trying to—"

Whatever Rosa had intended to say in Longarm's defense was knocked out of her by Trace. Through a veil of whiskey and pain, Longarm saw her fall, and when Trace came at him swinging, Longarm kicked out with his boot. It struck Trace in the hip instead of where it would have done some real damage. The outlaw leader cursed and hit Longarm twice more. After that, Longarm was tied to a big pine supporting column and his shirt was torn from his back.

"This man, whom I invited to enjoy our whiskey,

women, and food, held out two thousand dollars on us," Trace pronounced, looking at the excited faces of his followers. "I think that demands an extreme punishment, don't you!"

All except Noleta and Rosa shouted in the affirmative.

"Twenty hard lashes. One for every hundred dollars he held out on us seems about fair, doesn't it!"

Again, they all shouted that, indeed, the punishment should be at least twenty lashes.

When the first one cut into the flesh of Longarm's back, he thought he had been skewered by a red hot poker. His spine arched and his mouth flew open, but he did not cry out.

"One!" Trace shouted wildly and then his whip snuck out and cut deep into flesh a second time. "Two!"

Longarm bit into the cuff of his sleeve and locked his jaws shut. He was damned if he cried out and showed this man his pain.

"Three!" Trace and the crowd shouted in unison. "Four!"

Trace crowed, "Who wants to bet me that he screams by the time he gets ten and passes out before fifteen!"

Longarm didn't hear the response. There was a loud howling in his ears and his eyes were shut so tightly that all he could see was a red, swirling sea.

"Five!"

He slumped a little, then spit the cuff of his sleeve out and shouted, "Trace, if I live through this, I swear that I'll kill you!"

"Anger is good! Hatred even better. Here comes number six," the man cackled insanely.

"Six!"

When the whip cut into his back again, Longarm almost screamed. He clenched his teeth down and felt blood in his mouth where he must have bitten his tongue.

"Seven!"

Longarm wasn't sure that he could keep from crying

out or even that he could stay conscious. His mind was riding a bolt of fire that was consuming him, one body fiber at a time.

"Eight!"

Longarm had mercifully passed out somewhere between the fourteenth and the sixteenth lash. Now, he awoke in a bed lying on his stomach with Rosa sitting at his side, tears running down her cheeks.

"It's all right," he managed to whisper. "I'll pull through."

"Will you?"

"Of course," he said, wanting to vomit and then pass out again. "I'm still tough."

Rosa reached out and touched his cheek. "Your back is bloody. Trace might have killed you except that I threw myself on you and he began to laugh so hard that he could not swing the bullwhip anymore."

"Did he whip you too?" Longarm managed to ask.

"Only once . . . this time."

"I *will* kill him," Longarm vowed, breathing hard and digging his fingers into the bed's mattress. "There is no doubt about that."

"Trace would have killed you except that I reminded him that, if he did so, he would not know where the two thousand dollars was hidden."

Longarm closed his eyes. "That's something that I should have reminded him of myself. Thanks for saving my life, Rosa. I'll try to return the favor."

"Trace will forgive you now. He has shown everyone what will happen if they lie or cheat him."

"I'm glad that he forgives me, but that doesn't change the fact that he is a dead man once I get back my strength."

"Custis," she said, leaning close. "You must not say or even think that way. You must pretend to be afraid of Trace. If he thinks you fear him, you will be safe. But if you do not show him fear, he will surely have you killed."

"I fear him all right," Longarm admitted. "But I'll kill him just the same, and I'll see that you get out of Gunshot."

"If that is a promise, it is one that I will hold you to," she told him.

"It's a promise."

"I have coated your back with salve made by the Paiutes from aloe and other cactus. It eases the pain and quickens the healing."

"I don't know about the healing," Longarm told her, "but it doesn't seem to be doing anything for the pain. Can you get me some whiskey?"

"Yes." She already had a bottle.

"Don't lose heart," he told her. "Things can only get better."

"This is Gunshot," she told him. "And here, things *never* get better."

It took Longarm three weeks to begin to feel human again. In all that time, Rosa rarely left his side. She changed his bandages and brought him food, water, and whiskey. Sometimes, though, she had to go downstairs and be with other men. Once she was gone for longer than usual and returned with her lips all puffy and her eyes red from crying, Longarm sat up with alarm.

"What happened?"

"Trace wanted me again," she said, voice barely a whisper. "He was angry with Noleta and wanted to get back at her so he took me to his bed. She walked in when Trace was on top of me and they got into a fight. I got hit in the face, but Noleta got it even worse."

Longarm's blood began to boil. "What kind of a man is he?"

"He is not a man. He is an animal with no more feelings than a rabid wolf. It pleasures him to hurt and to kill. Everyone is afraid of him and does his bidding. Even me."

"I won't," Longarm vowed. "And the day is soon coming when I will kill him. When that happens, what do you suppose will become of the others?"

"Someone will try to take his place," Rosa said. "Men will fight among themselves to become the new boss. The strongest will win and nothing much will change."

"But it *will* change," Longarm insisted. "The law will come down on Gunshot."

"The law is afraid of this town," she argued. "Don't you think that the law has already tried to come here and put a stop to Trace and his gang?"

"I'm talking about the army."

"Once a patrol came from Fort Cannon."

"And?"

"They never even got close to Gunshot. They were attacked while riding through a canyon about twenty miles to the north. Not one soldier lived. Everyone died and they never tried to come back."

"I had no idea," he whispered, unable to hide his disappointment and shock.

"Why should you?"

Longarm realized he had come close to giving away his secret. "No reason," he told her. "It's just that you would think that something like that would have raised a lot of trouble for Gunshot."

"The army was humiliated and never said anything. But I know where the bones of twenty horse soldiers lay bleaching in the hot sun."

Longarm shook his head. Even Billy Vail had seemingly been unaware of this shameful massacre.

"Trace told me that he is about ready for you to take him to the place where you hid that two thousand dollars in bank money. He also told me that his men said that the robbery happened in a town called Durango."

"I see."

"I am afraid that, when you take him to the money, he will decide to kill you."

"Why would he do that?"

"Because you can't hide the fact that you are not really afraid of him. And that means you are a danger to Trace and must die."

"Maybe I'll kill him when we go to get that bank money," Longarm said. "Then I'll come back for you."

"If you kill him, you had better ride hard and fast," Rosa warned. "I would want you to come back, but not without many, many friends. Otherwise . . ." She did not have to finish because her expression told him what would happen.

"Is there anyone else in Gunshot who would like to see Trace dead besides ourselves?"

"Noleta."

"Yes, but I meant any outlaws?"

"There is one."

"What is his name?"

"Gavin. But he is young, and I don't think he is strong enough to help you."

"Could you talk to him?"

"If I do, he might tell Trace and my own life would be in danger."

"Then I'll find and talk to him," Longarm decided. "I remember him."

"Gavin is a good person," Rosa said. "He is like you. He made some mistakes."

"He killed his lover, her father, and another man," Longarm reminded her. "But all of them in self-defense. "That tells me that he is good with a gun."

"Maybe."

Longarm grabbed his boots. Up until now, he had forsaken wearing a shirt because of the scabs still healing on his back. But he could wait no longer and so he said, "I need a new shirt."

"I will get one for you," Rosa said. "If you talk to Gavin, please do not mention that I gave you his name."

The poor woman was actually trembling. And suddenly she broke down, covered her face, and began to sob.

Longarm sat down on the bed and gathered her into his arms. "It will soon be all right," he promised. "You have to believe me."

"I am trying. But after what happened to me a little while ago, I feel so dirty and rotten inside that I want to curl up and die."

"Don't do that," he told her. "It's not your fault. And Trace will pay for it with his life."

She looked up, eyes brimming. "You will not just run away first chance you get and forget about Rosa?"

"No. Never."

"I hope I can believe you, Custis."

"You can."

"Make love to me. Only that way can I feel clean again."

Longarm eased her back on the bed. Rosa was a pretty woman, but he did not really feel any great passion for her and that surprised him. Mostly, he felt tenderness and gratitude. But he understood her need and so he slowly undressed her, noting the dark bruises on her body where Trace had ravaged her in his rutting frenzy.

He began to kiss Rosa's breasts and soon, he felt aroused. She looked up at him. "I am so afraid, Custis."

"Of what I am going to do?"

"No, of what will happen to me if you are killed or don't come back to save me from this place."

Longarm eased her bruised, but still lovely thighs apart and gently made his entry. He shut his mind to everything, but how to make her feel good again as his friend and as a woman.

As the minutes passed, she began to respond. At first stiffly, then with mounting passion, until she was hugging him tightly and calling him her lover.

Longarm brought Rosa up to the crest of a powerful wave of thundering ecstasy and then, as gently as he could, he filled her with torrents of his own hot seed.

Later, she kissed his face over and over and thanked

him. Longarm did not quite know what to say. After all, not only had she saved his body from being torn completely apart by Trace's bullwhip, but she had given him her trust and her love.

He would repay her. Not only would he make sure that she was free of Gunshot, but he would give her some of Trace's money and see that she had a new start in life.

Chapter 11

Longarm went to the saloon looking for Gavin. The young man wasn't there, but Longarm tracked him down over at the livery where Gavin was saddling up to go for a ride.

"Well," the young outlaw said, his eyes frank and appraising. "I'm glad to see that you're up and around again."

"Thanks to Rosa."

"That was a terrible beating that you got from Trace . . . but I have seen worse."

"Did his other victims survive?"

"No."

Longarm inspected Gavin's horse. It was an Appaloosa with strong quarters and a deep chest. "He looks like he has stamina and can gallop forever."

Gavin smiled. "He can run for miles without tiring. He's not the fastest horse in Gunshot but, over a fifty mile race, I'd put him up against anything . . . even Trace's big sorrel gelding. You want to go for a ride?"

Longarm considered the invitation. "Why not? I've been cooped up in Gunshot too long."

"I get to feeling the same way. That's why I ride most days. Trace doesn't like that, but I do it anyway."

"What's his problem with a man going for a horseback ride?"

"He worries that someone in his gang might betray him. Might be meeting enemies or the law out there someplace. So I mostly just ride a big circle around town."

"He acts like the warden of a prison," Longarm said.

"That's right. How is your back?"

"It's almost healed. Still mighty sore, though."

"I'll catch your buckskin and bring him around. It'll do him good to get out and stretch his legs. It's bad for a horse to stand around all the time in a corral."

Longarm nodded and waited while Gavin brought his horse. Then he went into the livery and found his tack. He curried the buckskin and then saddled and bridled the animal. "All right, Gavin, I'm ready when you are."

"It's always good to ride straight through town first," Gavin explained, reining his horse onto the main street. "That way, Trace doesn't think we're trying to sneak off."

"Oh for crying out loud," Longarm swore. "Does the man think he owns everyone in Gunshot?"

"Yep."

Longarm was packing his gun and, if it hadn't been for Rosa and Noleta, he would have shot Trace on sight. But that would only get himself killed and certainly ruin any chance he had of helping those two captive women.

As they passed through town, Trace suddenly appeared. He leaned against a porch post and folded his arms across his chest, smoking a cigar. "Howdy boys," he called as they came abreast of him. "Out for a little fresh air?"

Longarm drew his horse up, and it took every ounce of self-discipline he could muster to say, "We are."

"Good to see you up and around, Custis. Now that you're feeling better, we'll soon be riding out to collect that two thousand dollars of bank money."

"Fine."

"I thought you'd say that," Trace told him, a smirk on his lips and those of a pair of men at his side. "Don't overdo it today, Gavin. I want to make sure that Custis is ready to go."

"Yes, sir."

They rode on aware that the eyes of many outlaws were upon them. Longarm saw Rosa and Noleta standing in the doorway of the saloon, but neither of them waved or smiled. To do so might have angered Trace.

When they were clear of town, Longarm said, "Let's take the kinks out of these horses."

"Good idea."

Longarm gave his tall buckskin its head and all he had to do was tap his heels lightly against its flanks before the big horse broke into a hard run. Longarm knew that his horse was fast and when he looked back, he could see that Gavin and the Appaloosa were eating his dust.

Longarm turned forward, a grin on his face. The air was cool and it felt good to be in the saddle again. His back didn't pain him at all and the racing gelding made his own heart pump fast.

On and on they ran until the buckskin began to slow. It was breathing hard after a mile and obviously not in top shape. That's when Gavin passed him on the Appaloosa as if he were standing still, making it Longarm's turn to eat a little dust.

"Whoa up," he said to his laboring horse, drawing it to a walk and then a halt. The buckskin lowered its head and sucked in big lungfuls of air. "I can see that you're not in much better shape than I am."

Gavin let his horse run another few hundred yards and then turned it in a big circle to return to Longarm. When he drew rein, his horse was still breathing easy.

"He's in great shape, isn't he," Gavin said with obvious pride.

"Top form," Longarm agreed.

"I take him out four or five times a week and run him about two, sometimes even three miles. I do that so—if the day ever comes when I just can't stand it any longer back in Gunshot—I can outrun anyone who comes after me."

"Even Trace and the sorrel?"

"I think so. He doesn't exercise his horse very often so it can't be in good shape. But, like I said, it's fast over the short haul."

"It's the long haul in life that always counts." Longarm studied the young man. "Life really is like a horse race."

"How do you figure?"

"Well, we win a sprint or two, but we all lose our share of races. However, it's the long run that counts. I mean that I've seen plenty of men and women that have had a lot of early success in their lives only to go to ruin in middle or old age. They lose everything they've accumulated. Money. Power. Prestige. It all falls apart, leaving them at the end of their lives old and embittered."

"Yeah, I've seen that too," Gavin said.

"Then you've probably also seen some fellas who made mistakes . . . serious mistakes early in their lives. But somehow, they learn from them and don't keep repeating those same mistakes. And then they start to right their past wrongs. Work a little harder and smarter. Pretty soon, that young man—even one that has done jail or prison time—he turns it all around and he becomes a respected and prosperous citizen."

Gavin's expression was troubled. "So is that how you hope it will all turn out for yourself?"

Longarm couldn't help but smile. "I hope to go straight and turn my life around."

"But you killed a *marshal*. And I've done even worse."

"You killed two men and a woman that were trying to kill you. You acted in self-defense, although I admit that on the surface it looks pretty bad."

" 'Pretty bad?' " Gavin laughed without humor. "My fate is sealed because I can't go back and try to explain. I have no witnesses to testify that I only tried to save my own life. I'd either hang . . . or be sent to prison for the rest of my life."

"Maybe not," Longarm told him. "An absence of witnesses can work both ways."

"I don't understand."

"Gavin, unless the prosecution can disprove your story . . . then the judge can choose to believe it. And, if you had a character witness or two . . . then you could get your name cleared and start out with a fresh chance at life."

"I've got no 'character witness,' " Gavin said bitterly. "I'd be lucky if a mob didn't break into the jail and string me up to a tall pine tree."

"I'd stand up and tell a judge that I believed you had no choice but to kill in order to defend your life."

"Well, since you murdered a marshal," Gavin said, "that's just not likely to happen."

"I guess not," Longarm said, still not quite willing to confide in this young man. "But I did want to talk to you about something besides horse racing and life."

Gavin tipped back his hat and turned his face to the sky. "Ain't those just about the biggest, puffiest, and whitest clouds you ever saw?"

"They're special all right." Longarm studied the kid and decided that there was a freshness and honesty that living in Gunshot hadn't yet wiped out. In a few more years, however, he'd have bet that Gavin would have become as hard and ruthless as the others in Trace's gang.

"What'd you want to talk about?" Gavin asked, looking at Custis.

"Rosa says that you're a lot different from the other members of the Gunshot Gang."

The mention of that woman's name brought a slight blush to Gavin's cheeks. "She said that?"

"Yes."

"Rosa is all right. I like her. I'm glad that she's taken a liking to you, but I have to admit that I've been kinda jealous. Not that I would rather it was me than you that took those twenty lashes ... but I would have liked to have had her play nursemaid to me that last three weeks."

"I can't fault you for feeling that way. Did you know that Trace raped and beat her up again yesterday?"

Gavin's smile died and his mouth twisted down hard at the corners. "That sonofabitch! I'd love to put a bullet in his brain."

"So would I."

"I expect that you would," Gavin said. "But if you did, he's got a lot of men around him who would kill you in a hurry."

"Maybe."

"No maybe about it."

Longarm frowned. "I believe that, once a cruel or murderous leader falls, his men have a choice. They can do his bidding ... or they can quit the game and give up. It's been that way all through history. That's why it's always been wise for the leader of an opposing army to try to kill his counterpart first. Once he does, the enemy often loses its resolve and its purpose no longer seems important. They now have a new choice."

"If you're talking about the men that Trace has himself surrounded with ... they'll never have a choice," Gavin said. "They're all wanted for murder. Their only choice would be the gallows so they'd never surrender. Make no mistake about that, Custis."

"When Trace and I ride out to get the two thousand dollars that was stolen by his brother, I'd like you to ride along."

"Why?"

Longarm knew he'd come to the point of no return in this conversation. "Because I'm convinced that we can kill Trace and whatever other men that he brings."

"That is the worst idea I've heard in a long, long time."

"Why?"

"Because Trace never leaves Gunshot with any less than ten gunslingers. And even counting ourselves in that

124

number, there is no way that we can kill Trace and the other seven."

"We could if we got the drop on them. Or maybe we'd only have to kill Trace and the others would run off."

"And you probably think that pigs will fly next week," Gavin said sarcastically.

Longarm studied the young man for a moment, then he decided to roll the dice and risk everything. "All right. I'm going to tell you something that you don't know."

"There is a lot I don't know."

"I'm not a wanted man. I'm a United States deputy marshal."

"What!"

"You heard me."

"I don't believe you."

Longarm had hidden his badge inside a secret cut he'd made inside one of his riding boots. It was a hiding place that had never let him down, and now he bent over and pulled the badge out of his boot top and flashed it at the astonished Gavin.

"Maybe you just stole that off the dead marshal you killed up in Laramie."

"Read it," Longarm ordered. "It's a United States officer's badge. I'm a federal marshal."

"But what about the wanted poster and the reward that's offered on you!"

"We print those up all the time in the Denver federal building."

"What's your *real* name?"

"It's Custis Long. I figured no one would know my name. I don't give it out in my work. I make the arrests and I ask all the questions."

Gavin removed his hat and shook his head. "I can't believe what I'm hearing."

"If you help me kill or capture Trace and his ringleaders, I'll testify to the judge up in Cripple Creek, Colorado, that I believe the charges against you should be dismissed because you killed only in self-defense. You were lied to and you were attacked and had no choice but to defend your life."

Gavin took a deep breath. "Lordy," he whispered, "I'm actually starting to believe you're telling me the truth."

"That's because you know the truth when you hear it. Gavin, how good are you with a pistol?"

"I'm damned good."

"Show me."

"You mean you want me to shoot something?"

"That's right. On horseback, I want you to draw your Colt and shoot . . . oh, how about that young pine?"

Gavin frowned. "It's got a real skinny trunk. Forty or fifty yards on a horse that might jump. Tough shot."

"Give it your best shot."

Gavin tied his reins and looped them over his saddle horn. Then, he drew his gun and it came up fast and smooth. The gun bucked five times in his hand. The Appaloosa stood as still as the Trojan Horse while long slivers of white wood and brown bark flew off the trunk of the pine.

"What do you think?" Gavin asked, glancing over at Longarm and being unable to hide his own satisfaction.

"Where'd you learn to shoot like that?"

"I've been practicing since I was twelve. I found me a great big gold nugget back then and didn't tell a soul that I spent it all on a pair of pistols and a couple of thousand rounds of ammunition. I shot it all up and used both guns until they were almost worthless. But by then, I was as good as any professional shootist . . . or so I figured."

"I see." Longarm pushed the brim of his own hat back. "To be honest, you're probably a shade quicker than most professionals. But the fastest isn't always the one that walks away from a gun battle."

"I know that. I've read about all the famous gunfighters. Billy the Kid. Doc Holliday. Wild Bill Hickok. I know

126

how they all lived and died. I also know that they always shot straight and steady."

"You got that right," Longarm agreed. "Gavin, there's little doubt that, between us, if we could get the drop on Trace and his bodyguards, we could either make them surrender . . . or gun them down."

"That would be extremely risky."

"You got a choice to make right now. Either agree with me or . . . I'm going to have to kill you."

Gavin's blue eyes widened with surprise. "But you're a United States marshal!"

"What other choice would I have but to kill you?" Longarm asked, hand slipping over to the butt of his gun. "If you choose not to help me, you'll tell Trace who and what I am. So are you with me . . . or against me?"

Gavin's eyes dropped to the smoking gun still clenched in his fist. "I might have a sixth round in the revolver. If I do, then I could kill you."

"Sure, then Trace might even make you one of his favored boys. You could ride with him and kill folks and rape women. But is that what you really want?"

Gavin said nothing.

"Or do you want to help me clean out Gunshot and help save Rosa and Noleta from ruination? And what about all the other innocent people whose lives we will be saving if we rid the Arizona North Rim country of this scourge?"

"All right, I'm in with you," Gavin decided, holstering his gun.

"Is it empty . . . or do you have a round left to fire?"

"I've got a round left," Gavin answered.

"Then use it and reload."

Gavin drew again and used his sixth bullet to shatter a little green pinecone into bits. Then he reloaded and turned his horse back toward Gunshot.

"Oh, one thing," Gavin said.

"What's that?"

"What if Trace doesn't want me to come along when you go to retrieve that two thousand dollars of bank money?"

"I'll figure out something if it comes to that." Longarm grinned. "So how much gold did you hold back from him?"

"What do you mean?"

"How much of Nellie's father's gold do you have hidden? You're too smart to have given it all to Trace and his friends."

"Maybe I didn't want to get twenty lashes with his bullwhip."

"That doesn't wash with me," Longarm replied. "It was inevitable Trace would find out about the bank robbery that got his brother and Dub Beason killed. Then he'd know that there was missing money. But the same can't be said for the gold you took from Nellie's father. So how much have you got hidden?"

"All right, it's at least a thousand dollars. Why are you asking? Do you want me to hand over that before you'll stand up for me to a judge?"

"Yeah. I want you to give it to a charity."

"Then I'll have nothing left to help me make a fresh start!"

"Wrong. Unless I'm badly mistaken, you'll have a clear name and a good chance at a successful future."

"Dead broke?"

"You're a smart young man," Longarm said. "Maybe even smart enough to marry Rosa and make her a respectable woman."

"You actually think she'd marry me?"

"She might."

"What about you?"

Longarm thought of Julie and Noleta. "I've got other plans."

"Yeah, I'll just bet you have," Gavin said with a grin. "All right, Marshal. If I survive, I'll hand over the gold in exchange for your helping hand with a judge in Cripple Creek."

"Fair enough."

"But I still don't give us more than about a one in three chance of surviving a shoot-out with Trace and his boys."

"One in three is better than nothing."

Gavin nodded as they started back to Gunshot.

Chapter 12

Two days later, Trace summoned Longarm and said, "It's time we recovered that bank money. I've waited long enough."

"All right." Longarm knew he should act contrite and fearful so he added, "Whatever you say."

"That's the spirit. We'll leave first thing in the morning. How long will it take to get to the hiding place?"

"Half a day."

"Good." Trace had been sitting beside Noleta, but now he said, "I'm glad that you're feeling better, Custis. And I hope there are no hard feelings on your part."

"Let's just say that I learned my lesson."

That answer seemed to satisfy Trace. He grinned at Noleta, then got out of his chair and came over to Longarm. Sticking out his hand, he said, "No hard feelings."

"No hard feelings."

"You just have to understand that I view Gunshot like a first-rate military commander would his frontier outpost. I'm the leader and I have to mete out discipline. We have rules and regulations in Gunshot."

"Yes, sir."

"Follow them and no one bothers you . . . but break the rules and you're punished. In the military, they send you

131

to the brig or stock house. Here, I have them tied to a post and then administer what, at least on the surface, might seem like an unduly harsh punishment. But it isn't."

"Twenty lashes isn't unduly harsh?" Longarm dared to ask.

"No," Trace said, steepling his slender fingers. "Actually, what you did by lying and holding out on your full contribution merited the death penalty. But I felt merciful and so your life was spared. I chose instead to make an example of you so that others would not try the same thing if or when the opportunity arose."

"I see."

"We'll go on patrol at eight o'clock tomorrow morning. I expect you to be saddled and ready to ride."

"Will we be going alone?"

Trace's eyes narrowed. "Now why would you ask such a question?"

"Just curious."

"You wouldn't be thinking of revenge, would you, Custis?"

"Of course not!"

"Good. There will be eight or ten of us. I like to keep my most loyal followers at my side. You're dismissed."

Longarm left the room and went to see Rosa, who was anxious about the coming day. "We're leaving at eight," he told the young woman. "Trace says that he has waited long enough to recover the bank money."

Rosa came to his arms. "He'll try to kill you after he has that bank money."

"Well then," Longarm said, pushing her out to arm's length and looking into her troubled eyes, "Gavin and I will just have to kill him and his henchmen first."

"What would your chances be?" Rosa shook her head. "Trace is very careful. He'll have his best gunmen with him tomorrow."

"I know that," Longarm said. "But we'll have the advantage of surprise."

"And what if he orders you to leave your weapons here in Gunshot?"

It was Longarm's turn to be surprised. "He'd do that?"

"Trace will do whatever he wants or thinks is necessary to protect himself against danger. He is a coward and a bully. He is also deadly, but prefers not to take chances."

"I see. Then I'll have to hide a gun in my boot or someplace," Longarm told her. "I already have a hideout derringer. I'll ask Gavin to do the same."

"I think you both will be killed."

Longarm took the frightened woman into his arms. "Rosa, listen to me. When we leave, you and Noleta prepare to go. What happens tomorrow at noon will create a huge diversion. If we are successful and kill Trace and his men, then we'll come back for you."

"But there will still be too many outlaws!"

"Then maybe we'll ride to Fort Cannon for help. Either way, we'll return and take you away."

"And if you and Gavin are killed?"

Longarm chose his words carefully. "If we are, it will not be before we've killed Trace and several of his men. When that happens, any survivors will be so shaken that you will still have a chance to escape. They'll be off guard and you'll need to leave tonight on fast horses. I'm sure that whoever is left will be so preoccupied with trying to assume control that your absence won't even be noticed until tomorrow."

"Where would we go?"

"Go to Fort Cannon and tell them that Gavin and I were killed, but that we killed Trace Hall, the leader of the Gunshot Gang. Tell whoever is in command there that they must attack and clean out this town while it is still in the grip of confusion and lack of leadership. Also tell the commander that my name is United States Deputy Marshal Custis Long."

"You are a federal officer of the law!"

"That's right."

133

Rosa hugged him tightly. "I *knew* that you were different from all the others. Is Gavin also a federal marshal?"

"No," Longarm told her. "He's just a good man who met a bad woman and let her take his life down the wrong path."

"I will tell the captain of the fort what you say. But please don't either of you get killed!"

"We'll do our level best," Longarm said, leading her over to the bed.

Moments later, they were locked together making passionate love.

Longarm managed to find Gavin that evening. The young man was out at the livery, currying his horse.

"I've been looking all over town for you," Longarm said, coming over to stand by the corral. "We're leaving at eight o'clock tomorrow morning."

"I know."

Longarm raised his eyebrows in question, but Gavin didn't notice so he asked, "How'd you know that?"

"Some of the boys told me."

"Were you invited to ride with Trace?"

"Nope." Gavin looked at him. "So I guess we'll have to think of another plan."

Longarm took a deep breath. "It's tomorrow or never. You and Rosa both know who I really am."

Gavin swung around and although it was dark, there was enough moonlight to see that he was upset. "Are you suggesting that either of us would tell Trace that you're a federal officer of the law?"

"No, but accidents do happen. Also, Trace will soon expect me to go out and break the law. To rob or to kill. So we have to take care of him tomorrow."

"But I already told you he's picked the men he wants to go, and I'm not one of them."

"Then follow us," Longarm urged. "I'll pick a spot out

134

in the open. When I dismount as if to go recover the bank money I've hidden, I want you to open fire with a rifle."

"Are you crazy!"

"They won't know it's you if you're hidden. They'll probably think it is a lawman or a vigilante committee. Just kill as many of them as you can and I'll be doing the same . . . starting with Trace."

"You'll be cut down among them."

"That's my problem, not yours."

"It's mine if they see me or follow my trail," Gavin argued. "Those men are professionals and you can bet they know how to follow tracks. If I come back here I'll be caught and tortured to death."

"Then don't come back," Longarm snapped. "You've already bragged about how that Appaloosa of yours can out leg anything here over a long run. Well, even if I'm cut down you'll still have the advantage of a big head start. Trace will be dead and the gang will be badly shaken and disorganized. Any survivors will just head for Gunshot and, by then, you'll be twenty miles away."

Gavin thought it over for a few moments then said, "What about Rosa and Noleta?"

"I don't know," Longarm confessed. "I told Rosa we'd be back for them if we killed Trace and his men. But if I'm gunned down, well . . . what happens to them is up to you."

"Oh no you don't!" Gavin protested, shaking his head. "I'm already carrying around a big load of guilt. I'm not going to take responsibility or guilt for their fates."

"Suit yourself. But what I'm offering you is a chance to get out of Gunshot. Maybe even a chance to clear your name if we can pull this off. Now what do you say?"

Gavin ran his hand along the Appaloosa's neck as he considered the request. Finally, he said, "I'll do it, but I'm far better with a pistol than I am with a rifle."

"Then instead of hiding and opening fire, you ought to charge forward and do some close in gun work."

"And be shot out of my saddle."

"Do what you want," Longarm told the young fugitive. "Just give me your word that you'll open fire as soon as I do. My first bullet will be for Trace. I expect to get at least three more of them before they recover. If you're helping me, we can wipe out every last one of Trace's bodyguards."

"I'll give you this much," Gavin said, "you're brave and amazingly confident."

"Maybe that's because I've been in a lot of gun battles. I've been shot, stabbed, beaten, and left for dead. Oh yeah, and I've also been horsewhipped half to death by Trace. But I always seem to find a way to survive and then win. And I don't see any reason why that should change with this bunch."

"I'll do what you say," Gavin promised. "So count me in."

"Good. But don't follow so close that they see you or we're cooked," Longarm told the young man.

"I won't. Why don't you remove your Stetson a few minutes before you climb down and open fire on Trace? That will give me a little bit of warning and time to move in closer."

"Then I take it you've decided to charge and use your pistol?"

Trace patted the Colt strapped to his hip. "It's what I handle best and you can bet I'll have a second gun loaded and ready."

Longarm nodded. "We've got a real good chance to make this work tomorrow."

"I know. But get Trace first. He's the fastest and most deadly."

"I will," Longarm promised.

"Are you going to actually take them to the place where the money is hidden?"

"I haven't decided yet," Longarm replied.

"Might be best if you did," Gavin said. "That way, if

something went wrong, you wouldn't be whipped half dead again. And mark my word, that's what will happen if your plan goes sour."

"My back and my pride won't take another beating like the last one. I'd rather go down in a blaze of bullets than allow Trace or any other man to slice my back open again."

"Don't blame you," Gavin told him.

Longarm figured that enough had been said. If someone saw him talking alone with Gavin out here by the horses, they might inform Trace, and he was a very suspicious man. No good could come of that.

"See you tomorrow about noon," Longarm said before walking away. "Don't let me down."

"I'll try not to."

Longarm left Gavin and headed back up the street. He figured that he and Rosa still had some lovemaking to do and, given what he faced tomorrow, it might be a good idea to get all the loving he could while he was still able.

But on his way back to the hotel to see Rosa, he was intercepted by Noleta, who whispered out of the shadows, "Custis?"

Longarm's first reaction was to draw his gun and whirl at the sound of her voice. But when he saw Noleta step out of the total darkness between two buildings, he held up and then reholstered. "You shouldn't have startled me like that, Noleta."

"I am sorry, but we only have a few moments and I have to speak with you."

Longarm heard the urgency in her voice and dragged her back in between the buildings, where it was almost pitch-black. He could not see the woman, but he could smell her perfume and, when he touched her, felt her tremble.

"What is it?"

"Rosa told me that you are a federal marshal."

"She shouldn't have said that."

"You can trust me, Custis. I only want to escape Gunshot, just like Rosa. And to do that, it is necessary to have your help."

"What are you talking about?"

"I think that Trace is suspicious of you already."

"Why?"

"Because one of his men—a bad fellow named Bart Hinton—says that he thinks he remembers you being a marshal. But Bart isn't sure. He said that you look like this marshal he saw up in Montana about five years ago. And he thinks that you and that man have the same last name."

Had he been alone, Longarm would have sworn out loud. Instead, he did so silently. "So what is going to happen?"

"I am not sure. Trace told me to leave while he talked to Bart some more. But I came looking to warn you."

Longarm considered this new and troubling development.

"Maybe you should try and get out of Gunshot right now," Noleta suggested.

"I don't think that would be a good idea. They'd come after me and they'd probably figure out that you were the one who told me I was suddenly under suspicion."

"Then we will *both* run away."

"And what about Rosa?"

"I could find her. If you could get us three fast horses, we would have a chance."

"Not much of one," Longarm said.

"Listen!" she said, panic rising in her voice. "I think that Trace will send men to hunt for you tonight. If they find you, they will tie you up and bring you to him. He might use the bullwhip on you again, and I could not bear to see that."

"I'll hide tonight and be ready with some answers at eight o'clock in the morning, when we are supposed to ride out. If Trace tries anything, I'll kill him on the spot and take my chances in a shoot-out."

"You'll have no chance."

"Then I'll just have to trust that this Bart fellow doesn't convince Trace that I was that Montana marshal. And besides, Trace probably won't do anything more until I hand over that two thousand dollars in bank holdup money."

Noleta hugged his chest in the darkness. "But wouldn't it just be easier if we all ran away tonight?"

"No," Longarm said. "We'd be hunted like a fox by the hounds and I doubt we'd get to Fort Cannon in time to be saved. That means that our best hope is just to play it straight and for me to show up tomorrow morning as if I had nothing but the bank loot to hide."

"All right then," she told him. "At least you have been warned."

"You've risked your life to save mine," Longarm told her. "I'm grateful."

"Help us," Noleta pleaded. "Don't get killed for you are our only hope to get away from Gunshot."

"It will all turn out fine," Longarm told her, trying to sound a lot more confident than he actually felt.

"Are you going to Rosa now?" she asked.

"Yes." He did not want to linger with this woman, for there was danger everywhere around them.

"Tell her to pray for us all."

"I will."

"Tell her that God will hear our prayers, even when they come from this earthly hell called Gunshot."

Chapter 13

Longarm arose early the next morning with Rosa still sleeping peacefully. They had made love often in the night and he knew that the woman was exhausted and needed rest, so he didn't want her to awaken.

Just as he was about to leave, however, she reached out for him. "Be careful, Custis."

"I will," he promised, strapping on his gun. "Keep the faith, Rosa. I think we're going to win. But either way, Trace is a dead man and you and Noleta need to leave as soon as possible tonight."

"All right. Give my love to Gavin. Tell him I will pray for him as well as yourself."

"I will," Longarm said on his way out the door. He headed straight for the livery before anyone else in Gunshot was up and about. When he arrived there, he saddled his buckskin and was just about to mount up when Gavin slipped out of the barn and said, "Hey, Custis?"

"Yeah?"

"Can we talk for a moment?"

"Sure," Longarm said, leading his horse over to the barn and squinting in order to see the shadowy figure. "What's the trouble?"

"I was wondering if maybe I should try to bring Rosa with me when I follow you and Trace."

"Why?"

"Because when the shooting starts, if you're killed and I'm still alive, I can just take her away easier than I could here in town."

"And what about Noleta?"

"I can't take care of everything," Gavin said, avoiding his eyes.

"Best have them remain here," Longarm decided. "What about you? No change of heart?"

"No. I said I'd be there when the shooting started, and I won't chicken out on you. But you got to promise me you'll help get that Cripple Creek judge to let me off the hook."

"I'll try," Longarm told the man. "But like I said earlier, I can't make any predictions or promises."

"Fair enough." Gavin expelled a deep breath. "Are you even a little bit scared of what will happen to us?"

"More than a little."

"Really?"

"Sure," Longarm admitted. "We'll have to kill Trace and then seven of his best gunmen. That's a tall order."

"You bet it is! But I think we got a chance. I really do. You're the one that stands the greatest risk. When you shoot Trace, try to dive for cover. I'll come running and shooting. I just hope I don't lose my grip and shoot wild."

"Dismount before you attack them," Longarm advised. "You're good and that's a fine horse you have, but no man is all that accurate from the back of a racing horse."

"All right." Gavin reached out into a shaft of sunlight. "Good luck to both of us," he said, shaking Longarm's offered hand.

"Yeah."

Longarm mounted his horse and rode up the street. Men were already starting to gather, for everyone knew that

142

this was to be a big day for Gunshot with two thousand dollars on the line.

Longarm tied the buckskin up and went down the street to where he had eaten before. He wasn't the first customer, and when he ordered a big breakfast, it was slow in arriving.

"Hey, gawdammit!" a big man with a full beard shouted from the doorway. "We're ready to ride."

"I'll be right there," Longarm told him as he finished his breakfast and then gulped the dregs of his coffee.

"Trace is gettin' madder by the minute!"

"Take it easy. I'm coming."

Longarm lit a cigar, and he didn't hurry as he walked outside. Sure enough, Trace was mounted and so were about eight of his toughest men.

Trace drew out his pocket watch and bellowed, "Get your dumb ass in the saddle, mister!"

"Sure," Longarm said, offering the man a smile that only seemed to make him more furious.

Rosa and Noleta were watching, and so was Gavin, as Longarm mounted his buckskin, then reined it around and headed down the street with Trace and the others falling in behind.

"What are you trying to do? Make me look bad?" Trace hissed as he rode up close to Longarm and leaned forward in his saddle.

"Nope."

"Well I don't wait on anybody!"

Longarm decided to say nothing. Instead, he put the buckskin into an easy gallop and they left Gunshot behind, heading east. He guessed they'd be riding well into the early afternoon before he came to the hidden money. He just hoped that Gavin would hold up his end of the showdown. Otherwise, Longarm knew that he only had a few precious hours to live.

Not much was said that morning as they rode east toward Colorado and then turned south toward Lee's Ferry, still a good distance to the south. Longarm thought about Rosa, Noleta, and Gavin, but not as much as he thought about Julie and the widows at Cozy Dell beside the Colorado River crossing. He wondered if Mrs. Huddle and Mrs. Evans, with her son Henry, had recovered from the tragedy they'd suffered. Just remembering that those killers and rapists had belonged to Trace's Gunshot Gang made Longarm all the more determined that he would kill the men who followed him now.

They stopped to rest the horses several times, and the temperature rose into the low nineties as they descended from the higher ground.

"There's a family down at Lee's Ferry that probably has something of value we could take from them," the man named Bart said, eyes ever probing Longarm as if he could read his mind.

"I know," Trace said. "Maybe we'll go on and pay them a visit. But I doubt they have much of value."

"There might be some other Mormons either crossin' the Colorado or visitin' them," Bart said. "Could be some younger women there we could pleasure ourselves with, boss."

"We'll see," Trace said. "I already got two pretty women to bed whenever I want."

"Yeah, but we could use some fresh girls," another man said, looking hopeful.

Longarm said nothing. As far as he was concerned, these men would never reach Lee's Ferry or any other place alive. He saw them as nine dead men, although that sounded pretty optimistic given the odds. But more than once in his law career, he'd bucked long odds and come out the winner. And, if Gavin arrived and didn't panic, Longarm thought their chances of survival were at least fifty-fifty.

"Let's ride," Trace grunted, grinding out his cigar under his boot heel. "I don't much care for this hot weather

144

down here in the low country. You boys are already smelling pretty ripe."

Longarm would have liked to remind Trace that he didn't smell like a rose himself as they climbed back onto their horses. He glanced back to the south, hoping to get a reassuring glimpse of Gavin, but saw nothing but empty space and lots of red rock.

If he's doing it right, I won't see him until I open fire on Trace and the others.

As the noontime passed and the heat grew ever more oppressive, Trace's mood grew even darker.

"Custis, are you sure you know exactly where you hid that money?" he demanded.

"Yeah, I know. A fella doesn't forget where he hid two thousand dollars unless he's stupid or drunk."

"You aren't drunk, but I don't know about the other," Trace said in a sarcastic voice.

By mid-afternoon, Longarm saw the place where he'd hidden the stolen bank money. It was buried under a pile of rocks that no one would give the least bit of notice. Fortunately, the rocks were located close to the trail and this section of it was in open country.

Longarm reined in his horse and removed his hat, praying that Gavin was watching and would take it as his signal to come in close and be ready to open fire.

"What the hell are we stopping for in this midday sun!" Trace snarled. "Let's ride."

Longarm raised his hat all the way over his head and acted as if he were stretching. He could feel Trace's eyes boring into his back.

"Come on!" Trace hollered.

Longarm replaced his hat and rode up to the pile of rocks. He dismounted, looked back over at Trace and his men, then said, "This is the place."

"Where?"

Longarm moved over to the pile of rocks. He wished the pile were higher so he could drop behind it and have

145

some protection, but the pile was only a couple of feet tall. "Right here," he said, heart hammering in his chest as his gun hand inched closer to the well-oiled Colt at his side.

Trace didn't dismount and neither did the others. Longarm waited for Gavin to open fire, but when he didn't, there seemed nothing to do but to make his play and kill the outlaw leader. Without Gavin's gun to back him up, Longarm knew that he was a dead man.

"Hey," one of the outlaws said, twisting around in his saddle, "here comes a goddamn kid!"

"He ain't no kid."

"Pretty much he is."

Longarm's hand was on the butt of his gun and he was ready to draw when he recognized—not Gavin—but young Henry Evans. What in the devil was that kid doing out here?

"Give me the cash," Trace said, then turning to his men said, "A couple of you boys go see what that kid is doing out here by himself."

Two of the outlaws whipped their horses into a hard gallop. Longarm wanted to go for his gun, but he couldn't risk having Henry shot up or taken captive. There was nothing he could do but take Trace's orders when Trace said, "Give me the damned money!"

Longarm tossed the rocks aside. *Where in blue blazes was Gavin and what was Henry doing up here!*

The bank money was just as he'd left it, and when Longarm lifted the heavy bag and handed it to Trace, the outlaw grinned and tore it open to grab handfuls of cash.

"Damn, this feels better than grabbbin' ahold of Noleta's breasts!" the man swore.

Longarm wasn't listening. Instead, he was watching as the two outlaws met up with Henry Evans. He saw them reach out for the kid's horse, trying to grab the reins out of his hand. Henry shouted something and it sounded like a cry of pain. Then there was gunfire and one of the outlaws sagged in his saddle. A moment later, there was a second shot, but it was impossible to see who was shooting.

"What the hell!" Trace cried, twisting around and gazing back toward the commotion.

"Hey boss, that kid is gettin' away!"

Longarm drew his six-gun just as Trace wheeled his horse around, shouting for everyone to catch the kid. He fired and saw Trace stiffen in his saddle and lean forward. He would have shot the man a second time and finished him off, but one of Trace's men spurred his horse forward. He blocked Longarm's aim, but took the second bullet in the chest.

Suddenly, Gavin burst out of the trees, opening fire with a gun in either hand. Then everything got crazy real fast. Gavin shot two of Trace's men and Longarm managed to knock another out of his saddle as Trace and the others raced away and found cover in the trees.

"What took you so long!" Longarm shouted as Gavin rode up and toppled out of the saddle, blood pouring from a wound in his side.

"You've been hit bad!" Longarm yelled as the outlaws began to return fire.

Longarm had no choice but to grab his young outlaw friend and drag him over to some bigger rocks through a hail of bullets. If Trace hadn't been hit, they'd probably have charged or at least gotten to their horses and used rifles. But Trace was wounded bad, just like Gavin, and nobody seemed inclined to charge into the battle.

Longarm looked down at Gavin, who was pale. "I've got to get you to a doctor."

"You know that there's no doctor within a hundred miles."

Longarm realized that Gavin was right. "Then I'll get you down to Cozy Dell and the women will have to save your hide. Why did you wait so long to attack!"

"I saw the kid riding up and knew he was going to

blunder right into the midst of the gunfight. I couldn't ride out and stop him without being seen, and that would have really put your life in danger."

"Do you think Henry escaped?"

"Yeah. I shot one of them that was trying to grab him and wounded the other pretty bad." Gavin closed his eyes, sweat beaded across his forehead. "I guess our little plan sort of went to hell in a handbasket, huh?"

"I guess," Longarm said, sending a couple of bullets in the general direction of the outlaws. "We have to get out of here and down to Lee's Ferry. You're in rough shape."

"Better than being dead." Gavin grinned. "Did they get the two thousand dollars?"

"I'm afraid so."

"Don't matter. We got away and you shot Trace, didn't you?"

"Yes, but he's probably in better shape than you are."

"Damn!"

Longarm saw Gavin's fine Appaloosa standing off to his left about twenty yards. "I'm going to grab your horse and bring him over here for you to ride. Think you can sit a running horse?"

"Hell no."

"Sure you can," Longarm argued. "You can do it until we get past those boys and are heading for the Colorado River."

"What if they come after us?"

"We'll face that one if it happens. Can you sit up and open fire when I make a break for your spotted horse?"

"I think so."

"Good."

Longarm helped Gavin into a sitting position and then stuffed his bandana into the man's wound to slow the bleeding. "Ready?"

"Don't get killed out there, or I'm a goner for sure," Gavin ordered.

"I'll try not to."

Longarm broke and ran for the Appaloosa. Fortunately, he was nearly out of pistol range from the outlaws and he made it without a scratch. He jumped onto the horse and rode it back to Gavin while errant bullets whined through the hot air.

"Let's get you mounted up."

Gavin clenched his teeth, and Longarm lifted him into the saddle. "Hang on tight."

"What choice do I have?"

"None."

Longarm swung into his own saddle and they rode hard as the outlaws fired their pistols. If even one had had the presence of mind to make a run for the rifle on his horse, the deadly game would have been over. But they all played it safe and very soon, Longarm and Gavin were chasing Henry south toward the river and the little Mormon sanctuary.

The outlaws didn't pursue them which, given that Trace was in pretty rough shape, was not surprising. They'd undoubtedly decided that their leader needed the attentions of Rosa, Noleta, or maybe even someone in their gang that had some medical training.

Trace carried a bullet in his body, but so did Gavin, and there was no way to know which of them might live or die.

Chapter 14

.

Gavin was in desperate shape by the time they finally reached Lee's Ferry late that night. Young Henry must have told everyone what he'd seen, because Caleb had everyone armed and ready to defend themselves from the Gunshot Gang if they'd chased Longarm.

"Thank heavens you're all right," Julie said, hugging him tightly. "I've been half crazy worrying about you!"

"I'm fine, but my friend is in bad shape."

"Let's get him inside," Caleb said, helping Longarm pull the wounded man out of his saddle, then carry him into their little house.

"He's got a bullet in his side that has to come out right away, or he's dead for certain," Longarm told the ladies.

"I've taken them out before," Mrs. Huddle said.

"So have I," Caleb's wife added. "But the man already looks half dead."

"He is," Longarm agreed. "But the bleeding has stopped, and I still think he has a chance."

"If we're going to extract a bullet," the Mormon woman said, "then let me clear the big dining room table and we'll lay him out there. Mrs. Huddle, please get a pot of water to boiling. Mrs. Evans, tear up some rags for bandages. We have to work fast."

Julie left Longarm and went to help the other women. Despite a long afternoon and evening of worry, she looked wonderful. Her arms were tanned and her face had filled out a little, giving her a softer, healthier appearance. Longarm figured that living with these good and hard-working Mormon people must have set well with his adventurous Denver mistress.

The women quickly began to make a place for Gavin on the big rough-hewn table that the family used at suppertime. Longarm went back outside with Caleb and Henry following on his heels.

"Henry, what in blazes were you doing out there this afternoon all by yourself?" Longarm demanded in a voice that carried only a hint of his real anger. "You ought to have known better than to have ridden so far from this settlement."

"I'm sorry."

"That doesn't answer my question."

When Henry began to stammer, Caleb jumped in saying, "Don't be too hard on the young man, Marshal. I'd sent him north to watch for the Gunshot Gang. He was on my best horse with orders to come running if he saw trouble heading in our direction."

Longarm expelled a deep breath releasing his anger. "Okay. But I think it was a mistake to send Henry out that far by himself. It nearly got us killed."

"A couple members of the gang passed through here a few days ago," Caleb said, his eyes solemn. "They were asking about some missing men, and I think they were looking for the four outlaws that you killed. That made us all pretty nervous here at Cozy Dell because they would likely have assumed *we* killed those four and then returned with more of the gang seeking retaliation."

"I understand."

Longarm began to unsaddle his sweaty and tired buckskin, but Henry said, "I'll take care of your horse and that Appaloosa, Marshal Long. And I sure am sorry about nearly getting you killed. That was the last thing in the world that I would have wanted, seeing as how you saved our lives."

"Forget about it," Longarm told the kid. "If young Gavin pulls through, there won't be any regrets the way it turned out."

"Did you kill the leader of them gawdamn murdering bastards?" Henry asked.

"Son," Caleb said with disapproval, "don't take the Lord's name in vain or use profanity. It's a sin, and we have enough to worry about without incurring His disfavor."

"Yes, sir. But, Marshal, did you?"

"I wounded him, but couldn't get a clear second second shot. I don't know how bad Trace is hurt, but I suspect he's in nearly as bad shape as that young man inside."

"Who is that man?" Caleb asked.

"He's a fella that made some poor choices and has paid for them. Gavin was a member of the Gunshot Gang until I recruited him to help me out."

"Is he a good, God-fearing man?"

"I know that he's good, but I'm not so sure about the other part," Longarm answered. "Even so, I am sure that it wouldn't hurt to put in a few prayers for him and for a couple of women that live in Gunshot."

"Harlots, most likely," Caleb snapped in an uncompromising tone of voice.

"As a matter of fact, they are fine women who are trapped in Gunshot and forced to endure a great deal of suffering and degradation. Both knew about our plan to escape, and I promised that I would deliver them from that lawless town."

"And exactly how," the Mormon ferryman asked, "do you propose to do that?"

"I mean to ride on to Fort Cannon and get the army to help."

"That's quite a distance."

"You have any better ideas?"

"No," Caleb said, "but neither do I have much faith in the United States Army."

"That's because your church and people have been at odds with our government for years," Longarm said. "The army never protected you from persecution back East, and they sure didn't help Brigham Young when he led your people out of Nauvoo, Illinois."

"And the government still refuses to help us," Caleb said with bitterness. "The commanding officer at Fort Cannon is Colonel Avery Blanchard. He's made it clear that he cares nothing about our welfare. Instead, he's concentrated on ridding this country of our Indian friends, the Utes and the Paiutes."

"I have contacts back in Denver who have their own contacts in Washington, D.C." Longarm grabbed a curry-comb and began to help Henry brush his sweat-caked buckskin. "If this Colonel Blanchard refuses to form a company and ride against Gunshot, I'll ask that he be immediately replaced."

"Do you think that would be possible?"

"I do," Longarm said. "My immediate superior in the Denver federal office sent me here to do a job. When I telegraph him that we need the United States Army, he'll see that it gets done if he has to go all the way to the top."

Caleb straightened. "There's a telegraph at Fort Cannon. But I imagine it would take quite a bit of time if Colonel Blanchard proves to be as stubborn and uncooperative as he has in the past."

"Perhaps it won't come to that," Longarm said. "At any rate, I'll ride out in the morning."

"Your horse is wore out. You can take our best saddle horse along with a second animal in case you come across the Gunshot Gang and have to make a run for your life."

"Thanks," Longarm said, "but I'll take my chances with these two animals. I'll ride steady, but not fast, until

154

we've climbed back out of this lowland. Just give me plenty of grain."

"Can I go with you?" Henry asked.

"I'm afraid not."

Longarm could see the wanting in the young man's eyes and now the disappointment. "Henry, it's not that I wouldn't like to have you along . . . because I would. It's just that, if the gang did come here with blood in their eyes, then you'd be badly needed to help protect the women and children. Gavin is exceptional with a six-gun, but he's in no shape to fight."

"All right," Henry agreed.

Longarm took some gunnysacks that Caleb handed him and wiped the buckskin's slick, wet coat down. He led the animal into a corral and went back to help Henry curry and rub down Gavin's fine Appaloosa. The reason he hadn't accepted Caleb's offer to use two of the Mormon's horses was that all of them were more suited to the plow than the saddle. Other than that, there was only the awful little pony that he'd delivered when they'd first arrived.

Because it was so crowded, Longarm took a light blanket and went out to the little peach orchard owned by the family. He spread the blanket out and went to sleep at once, but only a few hours later, Julie lay down by his side.

"I couldn't stand to be in there with you out here," she explained after giving him a big kiss. "I have missed you so much!"

Longarm drew her close, and she laid her head on his chest so that both of them could gaze up through the branches of the peach tree and stare at the stars. "I've missed you, too."

"Is there any chance you could take me with you to Fort Cannon?"

"I'm afraid not. I'm taking two horses and, if I'm

jumped by the gang, I'll need a relay animal to outrun them."

"Oh, that's all right. These are nice people, and I'm doing just fine here. Actually, I'm becoming quite a farm girl. They've taught me how to use the spinning wheel and how to card wool. How to milk a cow and a goat, and how to churn butter until my hands blister. I've planted tomatoes and cut hay for the animals. It's a hard life that these people live, but a good one."

"You look strong and healthy."

"Healthy enough to handle you," she teased.

Before Longarm could think of a reply, Julie was unbuttoning his pants and groping for his rod. She pulled it out and gave it a tweak, saying, "I expect this big fella has gotten kind of hungry, huh?"

He dared not tell her about Rosa as she worked his manhood into stiffness. Then, she bent over and took him into her mouth. Longarm sighed with contentment, and when he couldn't stand the fire in his groin any longer, he rolled Julie over and they began making love in the peach orchard. But when Julie's fingernails bit into his back, Longarm couldn't stifle an anguished groan.

"What's wrong!"

"It's my back. I . . . I was bullwhipped."

Julie pushed him aside and sat up, then raised his shirt to stare at the damaged flesh still scabbed and ugly even in the soft moonlight. "Oh, Custis, he really cut your back up something terrible!"

"It's nearly healed," he told her. "But I can tell you that things were kind of rough for the first week or two after that whipping. And it was all that I could do not to take my gun and shoot Trace."

She fell back, shaking her head. "I can't imagine what kind of a human being would do something like that. And for what?"

"It's a long story," he said, gathering her into his arms and pushing her back down on his rumpled blanket. Longarm mounted her again and soon they were slamming up and down so hard on the ground that he was surprised they didn't shake all the ripening peaches off their trees.

"Oh my," she gasped, then bit her knuckles to keep from screaming with pleasure.

Longarm took her fast and with great, unrestrained pleasure. Minutes later, they lay catching their breath, very well satisfied.

"Are you going to make it to Fort Cannon?" Julie asked, finally breaking a long, contented silence.

"Yes," he told her. "And I'm going to convince the commanding officer that he'll never have a better chance to rid northern Arizona and southern Utah of the Gunshot Gang than he will have during the next week, when Trace is either dead or badly wounded."

"What's he like?"

"He's like a rabid dog," Longarm answered. "I can't begin to tell you how much satisfaction I'll have to either finish him off or see him hang."

"And his men are all as bad?"

"They're as rough a bunch as I've ever come across. They are the worst of the worst."

"Do they have any women or children in Gunshot?"

"A few."

"Of which?"

"Women," he said, not wishing to elaborate.

"Poor things," Julie said.

"Yeah."

She curled up next to him and soon fell asleep. Longarm enjoyed holding her under the stars and, had he been in better physical condition, he'd also have enjoyed making love to her again before dawn. But he was exhausted and so he quickly fell asleep.

When Longarm awoke to the sound of a rooster crowing, Julie had disappeared back into the house. She was

157

obviously a bit uncomfortable about sleeping with him among religious and respectable women.

Longarm could smell bacon frying in the house. He washed his face in the water trough, then brushed the dirt and leaves from his clothing and rolled the blanket before going into the house to see all of the women bustling around in the kitchen.

"Mornin' ladies," he said in greeting. "How is my friend, Gavin?" he asked, looking toward a screened off portion of the small house filled with humanity.

"He's doing much better. We got the bullet out of his side rather easily, thank heavens," the Mormon woman said. "I think he's going to make it just fine."

"That's great news," Longarm said, stifling a big yawn. "A cup of coffee would sure be nice."

"We can't drink coffee. It's against our Church's teachings."

"I forgot."

"But I can pour you a cold glass of buttermilk."

"That would be fine," Longarm said, mustering what passed as his best early morning smile.

"Hi," Julie said, looking guilty as sin. "Did you sleep all right?"

"Mostly. I woke up for something but forgot what it was. Hmmm, seems like—"

She cut him off with an anxious smile. "It's going to be another warm day, and you've got a lot of miles to ride. The bacon and biscuits are almost ready."

"Thanks," he said, hating himself for being so mischievous.

Caleb had been outside feeding the stock, and now the man shuffled in and sat down at the table to join Longarm at breakfast. "Did you have a good night, Marshal?"

"Sure did!"

Longarm's answer was so enthusiastic and Julie's cheeks were turning so red that the Mormon turned his full attention toward the food on his plate. They ate in silence, and when Longarm was finished, he went over to stand beside Gavin's bed. The handsome young man's color was much improved, and his breathing was now slow and steady.

Turning around, Longarm said, "You ladies did a fine job and are to be commended."

"We do what we have to do," Mrs. Huddle said.

Longarm excused himself and went out to saddle the horses. Henry had anticipated this, and the young man was already waiting. "Marshal," he said, "I sure would like to come along with you to Fort Cannon."

"We've been through that already, Henry. I told you why you were needed more here."

"I know, but I just have a feeling that you might run into trouble and need my help. Caleb and my mother both say that I can go with you if you agree."

"I'm taking two horses."

"I've got the ones that the dead outlaws were riding when you killed 'em. They're up in that little canyon, and it wouldn't take but a few minutes to catch and saddle them."

Longarm relented. The Gunshot Gang had never attacked this ferry before, most likely because they relied upon it to do their raiding down in New Mexico and the southern part of Arizona. That, and the fact that Trace was either wounded or dead made it even more unlikely that these good people would be attacked without provocation.

"All right. Go get those saddle horses and hurry up about it."

"Yes, sir!"

"And you better bring at least a pistol along for protection."

"I will, Marshal Long!"

The boy ran like the wind up the canyon while Longarm went to sit on a log. He found a stogie in his shirt pocket and a match. The sun was just coming up over the high red cliffs and soon this canyon would be awash in blinding sunlight. Longarm watched as Liam and some of the Mormon children came out to do their morning chores. The rooster was still crowing and it looked as if it was going to be a nice, warm and peaceful day.

When Henry was saddled, armed, and ready to ride, his mother came out with the other women. They packed the saddlebags with extra biscuits and some not-quite-ripe peaches that reminded Longarm again of the pleasure he'd had with Julie only a few hours earlier.

"Gavin says that you're not to worry about him," Julie told Longarm. "He says that he's going to be just fine here with four women tending to his every need."

"Get him up and working at something as soon as he's able," Longarm told her. "And watch out for him because he has a roving eye."

"Are you jealous?"

"Nope."

Her smile faded. "I'd hoped you were. But be careful anyway."

"Count on it."

Henry got a long list of instructions from his mother. Mostly they centered around the fact that, if they ran into trouble, they were to run and not fight.

"I promise I will," the young man said, looking embarrassed by his mother's concern.

"Let's ride," Longarm said. He glanced at Caleb. "What did you say was the name of the commanding officer at Fort Cannon?"

"Colonel Avery Blanchard. You won't be impressed."

"I don't need to be," Longarm said. "So long as he agrees to let me lead him and his soldier boys on to Gunshot."

Caleb started to say something, but Henry put his heels to his mount and Longarm's buckskin broke into a gallop. Tied to a lead rope not far behind was Gavin's powerful Appaloosa.

They'd taken their time climbing out of the great canyon and up to higher ground. Henry knew exactly how to reach Fort Cannon because he and his ill-fated family had stopped there on their way south before being ambushed.

"It ain't much of a fort, Marshal. No log walls around it or anything."

"How many soldiers do you think are stationed there?"

"Maybe fifty."

"That's enough to handle the job at Gunshot," Longarm told the kid. "I've whittled down the gang's numbers pretty good already."

"I don't have much respect for soldiers," Henry added. "Most of them are misfits unable to find work anyplace but in the army."

"I've known some fine officers and soldiers," Longarm replied. "And I've known some as worthless as those you mentioned. But mostly, they're good men. They'll need to be if we're to rid this country of the Gunshot Gang."

"These soldiers look pretty rough," Henry told him. "They don't wear uniforms much at the fort, and they don't shave, either. And when you get downwind of 'em, they stink pretty bad."

"Sounds like this Colonel Blanchard has let things go under his command," Longarm said. "That's unfortunate."

"I didn't like the way they looked at Mrs. Evans much, either. They looked at her like a man would a horse he was thinkin' of buying."

Longarm had no comment to that remark. But what the young man was telling him was discouraging, to say the least. It sounded as if the soldiers at Fort Cannon were almost as motley as Trace's gang of outlaws.

That night they camped up in the high country. Longarm doubted there was anyone within fifty miles, but he figured the wise thing to do was to have a cold camp.

"No fire," he told Henry.

"Yes, sir."

They'd hobbled the horses and let them graze in a mountain meadow. Up here the air was far cooler and more refreshing. They fell asleep under a blanket of stars and awoke feeling a definite chill in the air.

"It'll snow up here pretty soon," the young man said.

"We'll be long gone by then. How much farther do you think it is to Fort Cannon?"

"Maybe forty miles."

"More uphill?"

"No," Henry said, "There is some climbing, but also some goin' down. We brought the wagons through this valley. I remember my pa talking about how we were going to find some real good land to farm down south."

"I'm sorry about that. Were you close friends?"

Henry frowned. "No, I wouldn't say that. Pa was the boss, and I did what I was told or he'd put a switch to my tail. At least, he used to. But the last couple of years we worked together doin' whatever had to be done. Pa didn't talk much. He just worked and minded his own business. He was a good man, Marshal Long."

"And I'm sure he'd be proud of you knowing that you'll follow in his footsteps."

"I hope I can.

"You will."

"Do you think we'll get into a big gunfight with that gang?"

"Yes. But there will be enough soldiers to win the day, and I wouldn't want to risk losing you and then having to face your mother."

"Well, sir, my mother told me that the reason I could come with you was to help put an end to the killings. She said she couldn't bear the idea of more women losing their husbands and having to suffer the way that she and Mrs. Huddle suffered."

"I see."

"So she wants me to fight."

"Then I guess you will," Longarm said. "You're packing a side arm."

Henry drew the gun out of its scratched old holster. "It belonged to Pa, but it ain't much of gun, is it?"

Longarm reached out and took the weapon. It was an old Navy Colt .36 caliber, black-powder pistol that looked as if it hadn't been fired in years. "I've got a better extra in my saddlebags that you can have."

The boy frowned. "Thank you very much, sir. But I thought maybe it would be fitting to use Pa's gun. If I could kill someone who killed him then it would sort of be like a rightful justice, if you understand my meaning."

"Your pa would want you to go into a fight against professional gunmen as well armed as possible. That old Navy Colt has seen its better days and ought to be retired. Put it in your saddlebags and take the more modern weapon that I'm offering."

"You think I should?"

"I *know* that you should and that it's what your pa would also insist upon."

"In that case, I'll do it."

Longarm got one of the firearms that he'd taken off a dead outlaw and made sure it was loaded. "That will stand you in better stead than the old Navy."

"Yes, sir."

"But Henry, if you are bound and determined to come into the fight, you have to do exactly what I say. Is that clearly understood?"

"Yes, Marshal Long."

"I'm being paid to mete out justice and so are the soldiers. But you're not. Do you see the difference?"

"No, sir. They and their friends killed my pa and Mrs. Huddle's husband. And I know that they did even worse to my mother and her while I was hit and trying to help. That's why I got to get into this fight and not hold back even a little."

Longarm wanted to argue that point and again remind

163

Henry that he was all that his mother had left in her family. But Henry Evans had a look in his eyes that indicated he would not compromise when it came time to avenge the death of his father and the rape of his mother.

And Longarm realized that, if he were in the boy's shoes, he'd feel and act exactly the same way.

Chapter 15

Fort Cannon was just as run-down, unmilitary, and de-moralized as Henry had warned. It was nothing more than a collection of dilapidated log cabins that surrounded a weed patch that Longarm supposed had originally been the parade ground. There were no sentries on duty, and when Longarm rode into the fort, most of the men he saw were either asleep in rocking chairs or hammocks, or else playing cards or horseshoes.

"Can you tell me where I can find Colonel Blanchard?" he asked a group of soldiers that were pitching horseshoes.

A sergeant with a silver and black beard, who was dressed in leather breeches, red suspenders, and an army tunic graveled, "The colonel is in that big cabin with the porch. But it's his nap time and you'd best not disturb the man."

"When is his 'nap time' over?" Longarm asked, not bothering to hide his contempt.

The sergeant winked at his fellow soldiers, then pitched a ringer before he answered. "Colonel Blanchard usually sleeps until five o'clock, and then he gets fed. If you want to see him, you'd best wait until morning. That's when he's generally able to see visitors."

"What I have to say won't wait." Longarm's cold stare raked the sergeant and the other soldiers. "What kind of a pathetic military post is this?"

The sergeant's smile faded. "For your information, Fort Cannon don't get much attention from the brass back East. And it don't get any money for improvements, as you can guess from lookin' at the barracks and the other fallin' down buildings."

"Money or not," Longarm said. "This place is a mess. You men ought to be fixing up what you have and showing some pride in being soldiers. Isn't there any discipline here at all?"

Longarm had said this loud enough to be heard by most everyone lounging around the post, and from their expressions, it was obvious that he wasn't going to win a popularity contest. The sergeant in particular seemed to take offense.

"Mister," he said, "I don't know who the hell you think you are, but we don't appreciate someone spoutin' off at the mouth. This is a hard, dangerous country, and we all earn our miserly army pay."

"Not from what I can see," Longarm said.

"Maybe you'd like to step down from that buckskin horse and show me if you got something besides a big mouth."

"I need to see your commanding officer."

"And I told you he's not up to seeing visitors right now," the sergeant said, jaw tight with anger.

Longarm started to rein his horse around the man, but the sergeant blocked his path. "You and your young friend had better leave Fort Cannon."

"I'm not leaving and I'm not waiting."

"Troopers Smith, Winslow, and McLeod!" the sergeant shouted. "Get your weapons and come here on the double!"

Three soldiers went into their barracks and hurried back outside armed with carbines. "We got a problem, Sergeant

Veek?" one of them asked, weapon pointed in Longarm's direction.

"We do," Veek said, glaring at Longarm. "Unless this big fella has more brains than he's showed so far."

"Sergeant," Longarm said, "I'm starting to lose my patience."

Veek laughed, then glanced over at Henry. "Young fella, unlike your friend, you're awful quiet. You also look familiar."

"That's because my family came through here in a covered wagon last month."

"Now I remember. What happened?"

"We didn't make it all the way to Lee's Ferry," Henry answered, his voice thickening with pent-up emotion.

"We all got the right to change our plans," Veek said, hands on his wide hips. "But I can't say as I care much for the company you keep."

"He's a United States marshal and he saved my ma's life. He saved another woman, too!" Henry said between clenched teeth. "And he did it by killin' more outlaws than you or this dirty bunch of soldiers have ever even seen!"

Sergeant Veek's eyes widened. He turned back to Longarm. "Did you tell that young fella that you're a marshal?"

"I did because I am," Longarm said. He started to reach into his boot top, but the three armed soldiers aimed their weapons, thinking that he was reaching for a gun.

"At ease!" Longarm snapped. He drew his badge out of his boot top and showed it to the sergeant. "I've been sent here to clean out the Gunshot Gang. That's why I have to speak to your commanding officer right now!"

Veek stared at the badge, then took a closer look at the man holding it. "Listen," he said finally, dropping his horseshoes and wiping his hands on his dirty leather breeches. "Maybe we just got off on the wrong foot."

"Yeah," Longarm said, reining his horse around and riding over to the largest of the cabins.

"I'm telling you, Marshal," Veek said, following him. "Colonel Blanchard doesn't want to be disturbed in the afternoon!"

"That's too gawdamn bad," Longarm said, dismounting and tying his horse up to the rail in front of Blanchard's cabin.

"Suit yourself," Veek snapped. "Go ahead and wake the colonel up and see what *that* gets you."

"I will." He glanced over at Henry. "You stay here with the horses while I have a talk with Colonel Blanchard."

Longarm opened the door and stepped inside. All the curtains were drawn and the room's interior was dark and musty. He heard loud snoring and asked, "Colonel Blanchard?"

There was no reply. Only the snoring. Longarm walked over to a window and pulled back the curtain. Light flooded the room and a man stopped snoring, then belched and grunted. Longarm turned to see a very large, very disheveled army officer sound asleep, unpolished black boots resting on a cluttered desk, corpulent body tilted back in his leather office chair. He probably was in his early sixties, although he might actually have been ten years younger and prematurely aged by dissipation. Dressed in his much-too-tight officer's uniform, Longarm knew at once that this was Colonel Blanchard and that he was a bad drunk.

An almost empty whiskey bottle sat on the desk and beside it was a water glass, still unemptied of its amber contents. Blanchard roused momentarily, only to fall back into a drunken stupor, head sagging down on his great, blubbery chest.

"Well," Longarm said aloud, "at least the root problem is now obvious at Fort Cannon."

He surveyed the colonel's combination living quarters

and office. The place reeked; Longarm counted four empty liquor bottles in the trash.

So what am I going to do now? he wondered.

Sergeant Veek appeared in the doorway looking upset. "I tried to tell you that the colonel wouldn't be any use until tomorrow morning."

"How long has Blanchard been like this?"

"His wife died last year and he climbed into the bottle. We're just trying to keep him from losing his military pension."

"How long has he got to go?"

"He's eligible for retirement the end of this year, same as I am."

"And what's *your* excuse for letting things go to hell?"

To his credit, Veek was honest. "Truth is, Marshal, I like playing horseshoes and cards better than drill and hard soldiering."

"That's not good enough."

"Listen," Veek said. "You have to understand that Fort Cannon means absolutely nothing to the military brass back East. They don't care about us and we don't care about them."

"So you just take your pay and don't do a damn thing to earn it?"

Veek turned his head. "I've been a soldier all my life. Fought for the Union and was wounded twice. I fought Indians and I fought outlaws. I figured I've earned the piddling pension they'll give me and Blanchard at the end of December."

"Take me to the telegraph office," Longarm ordered. "I need to send a message to Denver."

"What kind of message?"

"That's my business."

"If you're using one of my men to send the telegram and you're using our equipment, then it is army business and that means that it's also my business."

"Sergeant, don't throw away your precious pension by

messing with something that you shouldn't. As far as I'm concerned, the negligence here falls squarely on Colonel Blanchard's shoulders. He is the one responsible for what I've found here, although you certainly ought to have done better."

Longarm stepped around the man and walked over to his horse so that he could speak to Henry. "The colonel is drunk. He's not going to be any help."

"What are you going to do?"

"I'm going to telegraph my boss in Denver . . . tell him what I need and the situation here, then let them decide."

"Marshal, I don't think you should do that," Veek said, coming up behind him. "Colonel Blanchard was a Civil War hero. He's earned his pension. Getting him thrown out of the army less than six months short of retirement wouldn't be right."

Longarm turned on the man. "Sergeant, I need help cleaning out Gunshot. I need the help of the United States Army and I will have it, unless I'm sadly mistaken."

"We already lost a lot of soldiers trying to clean out that bunch."

"So I heard. When?"

"About five months ago."

"Let's see," Longarm mused, "that would be just about the time that Colonel Blanchard's wife died."

"Just about."

"Take me to your telegraph office."

"I won't do that."

Longarm looked past the man. "I can see where the wires run. I can find it myself."

But Sergeant Veek planted himself in front of Longarm. "I can't let you ruin the colonel's career."

"You can't stop me."

"Oh yes I can. All I have to do is summon my men and command them to throw you in the stockade."

"That would be a very, very bad mistake," Longarm said, wondering if Veek was foolish enough to destroy his own military career. "Because you'd lose your pension along with Blanchard. And besides that, some people living in Gunshot that are very important to me are counting on our help."

"Only the scum live at Gunshot."

"You're wrong. Think very carefully, Sergeant. Do you want to throw your pension out the window trying to protect a man that has obviously given up not only on himself . . . but also the army?"

Veek avoided the question. "Colonel Blanchard was a good commanding officer up until the last few months. He's got commendations and medals to prove it. Marshal, being an officer or a soldier is a hard, thankless job."

"I know," Longarm agreed. "I served my time during the war between the states just like you and Blanchard. But that didn't give me the right to steal the government's pay."

Veek looked past Longarm into the room at his Colonel. "Maybe we could work something out here."

"Like what?"

"I'll sober him up. I'll talk to the colonel myself. I'll see if he'll help you by sending me and my men to Gunshot one more time."

"I don't know," Longarm hedged.

"I promise you that tonight he'll be sober. And when Avery is sober, he's a damn fine man worthy of being an officer. Marshal, my commanding officer has spent his entire life serving his country and he deserves a chance to finish out his service honorably."

Longarm heard the pleading in Veek's voice and understood that he was a loyal soldier who loved his commanding officer and who desperately wanted to help him receive a pension and honorable discharge from the United States Army.

"All right," Longarm agreed. "Now put your men to work cleaning up this barnyard."

"What?" Veek didn't understand.

"Sergeant, you're collecting the taxpayers' money every time you get paid. So are these soldiers. So put them to work and do it now!"

"And if I do that and get the colonel to talk to you this evening at dinner?"

"It all depends on what he says," Longarm replied. "If Blanchard wants to do his duty and help me . . . then things might work out. But, if he doesn't . . . I don't care how many battles you and he have fought. Or how many medals you've won. I'll see that you both are given dishonorable discharges. Is that crystal clear?"

"Yes, sir!"

Longarm watched Sergeant Veek straighten, then turn and march back toward his men. He heard the sergeant roar out orders and then he saw the confusion of men too long accustomed to idleness. But by the time that Longarm returned to Henry and his buckskin, order was established and men were scrambling to grab hoes, rakes, shovels, and brooms.

"What happened?" Henry asked, looking amazed at all the sudden activity.

"I had to remind them that they are all United States soldiers. That they work for our government . . . just like I do."

Henry shook his head. "I never seen men jump to work so fast."

"There's no leadership here at Fort Cannon. No discipline or self-respect. I've never seen anything so bad at an army fort."

"They look willing and able," Henry said.

Longarm wasn't sure that he agreed with that assessment. "Oh, they know how to jump to an order. But can these soldiers ride hard and shoot straight? That's the *real* question."

Chapter 16

Longarm had waited patiently until early evening, when Sergeant Veek appeared in proper military uniform and gravely announced, "Colonel Blanchard will see you now."

"All right." Longarm looked to his young companion. "Henry, let's go see what the colonel has to say."

But Veek shook his head. "Just you, Marshal. The young fella can eat with us in the chow hall."

"Henry, are you hungry?" Longarm asked, knowing the answer.

"Starved!"

"Then eat your fill," Longarm told him as he headed off to meet the colonel.

When he entered Blanchard's combination home and the fort's headquarters, it was as if he'd never seen it before. The windows had been opened and the room had been freshened and was now flooded with sunlight. Everything was clean and orderly, including the colonel who sat behind his desk. Blanchard had shaved and, although his eyes were bloodshot and reflected his sadness and suffering, the man appeared alert and sober.

"Marshal Long," Blanchard said very formally as he

rose from behind his desk. "Sergeant Veek tells me that you need assistance at Gunshot."

"That's correct."

"Please have a seat." Blanchard motioned for him to sit in a chair facing the desk.

Longarm removed his hat. When Colonel Blanchard offered him a cigar, he accepted, and when the man lit a match, he saw how terribly the colonel's hand shook and realized that his body ached for liquor.

"Marshal Long, I'm afraid that we can't help you."

Longarm curbed a sudden flash of anger and lit his own cigar. "And why is that?"

"Our prime responsibility is to assist in the Indian problem. As you may or may not know, Fort Cannon was built and is funded in order to minimize the friction between the heathens and the whites."

" 'The heathens'?"

"The Indians. Ute. Paiute, and a few troublemaking Navajo that leave their reservation to steal Mormon livestock. It's not an easy task and it takes most all of our resources and manpower to handle these little incidents and keep the peace."

Longarm smoked for a moment, eyeing this wreck of an officer through a blue cloud of cigar smoke. "I understand," he finally replied. "But I must ask you to reconsider."

"I only wish that I could," the colonel said sounding regretful.

"No you don't. You see, I know about the soldiers that you've already lost trying to rid this country of the outlaw gang living at Gunshot. And given that fact, I can understand your reluctance to—"

"That has absolutely nothing to do with why I can't help you!" Blanchard shot back.

"Sir, it has *everything* to do with it," Longarm insisted, voice hardening. "Colonel Blanchard, I'm not going to beg you to join me and lead your troops against the Gunshot Gang. Instead, I'm just going to ask one more time, and if you refuse, I'll telegraph my immediate superior, who will in turn telegraph *your* superior in Washington, D.C."

Longarm had no idea if this would happen, but it sounded pretty good. He shrugged as if the choice that Blanchard made was of no great importance to him either way, then added, "I would also very much regret having to inform Washington that Fort Cannon is a military disgrace and in a state of unreadiness due to lack of leadership."

Colonel Blanchard's fat cheeks blew out like a bellows, and he struggled to his feet. "Marshal, that is an absolute lie!"

"No it's not. But what happens here is not my concern. I've been sent to take care of the problem in Gunshot. For your information, I've already been there. I know how many outlaws we have to kill or arrest and that we can complete the job with the help of Sergeant Veek and your soldiers."

Blanchard was livid. He swung around and faced the window, cheeks puffing in and out as he struggled for control. One of his meaty fists was clenched and he was smoking fast.

"Shall I go to send a telegraph?" Longarm asked. "If you order me not to do that, I'll leave at once and, if necessary, ride all the way to Cortez or Grand Junction to report that you refuse to cooperate and therefore need to be replaced."

"You're only a marshal," Blanchard said, swinging around and glaring across the top of his desk. "How dare you threaten me!"

"No threat." Longarm came to his own feet, placed his palms flat on the colonel's desk, and said, "It's just my promise to see that you're replaced as commanding officer of Fort Cannon. What happens to you after that is none of my concern."

"I . . . I could have you arrested!"

"Yes, I suppose you could. But that would only create more misery for you. Colonel, I'm not asking you to join me and lead your men against the murderers, rapists, and thieves in Gunshot. You can stay here dead drunk for all I care. But I do need Sergeant Veek and your soldiers."

Blanchard began to quiver. His face turned dark, and Longarm thought for a moment that the man was going to suffer a stroke of apoplexy. However, Blanchard somehow managed to gain enough self-control to stammer, "I . . . I led a charge at Gettysburg. I was at Shiloh, too! If my men go to fight, you can be very sure that I will be leading them . . . not you. Not even Sergeant Veek! Is that clearly understood?"

Longarm almost smiled. "Yes, sir."

"Good. Then forget about this telegraph business and join me for supper. We'll talk about what you have seen and discuss possible strategies. Agreed?"

"Agreed."

Colonel Blanchard stabbed his cigar into a huge brass ashtray then marched stiffly around his desk and out the door. Longarm followed, feeling much more hopeful than he had a few minutes earlier.

The next morning, Colonel Blanchard awoke without his usual hangover. He shaved, bathed and dressed in his finest uniform, then stepped out onto his front porch and shouted, "Sergeant Veek!"

"Yes, sir!" The man came running, and when he realized that Blanchard was not only upright, but shaved, clean, and sober, he grinned and snapped a salute to his commanding officer.

"Sergeant," Blanchard said, "I want an assembly of all the troops at noon today for inspection."

Veek's eyebrows shot up in surprise, but he managed to ask, "Mounted, sir?"

"Yes, of course! I expect spit and polish. Is that clear?"

"Yes, sir!"

Longarm and Henry were among those who overheard this startling announcement. "What did you say to Colonel Blanchard?" Henry asked.

"I just told him I expected his full cooperation. Otherwise, I'd see that he got sacked . . . and by that I mean kicked out of the army."

It was Henry's turn to react with surprise. "You could do that to a colonel?"

"No," Longarm admitted. "But the people I work for could shake things up all the way to the United States capitol and get results."

"Wow! Does this mean that they're gonna help us wipe out Gunshot?"

"I'd say so," Longarm told his young friend.

Longarm, Colonel Blanchard, Henry, Sergeant Veek, and fifteen cavalrymen left Fort Cannon the next morning. Each soldier carried an Army Colt revolver, a Springfield carbine, one hundred rounds of .45-caliber ammunition, half a two-man pup tent, rations for five days, a blanket, and a rubber sheet to be spread on the ground in good weather or to be spread over them in the event of rain. There were no artillery pieces at Fort Cannon anymore. They had been confiscated and sent to other forts deemed more worthy. But even if they had had artillery, both Longarm and Colonel Blanchard had agreed that it would be too slow and cumbersome to transport; swiftness and the element of complete surprise were crucial to their success against Gunshot.

On the second day out, they passed the canyon where Blanchard's soldiers had died in ambush. Sun-bleached bones were collected and buried with honors and a prayer. Even more grim and determined by the reminder of the good cavalryman already lost to the outlaws, their military patrol pushed on to the higher, greener country; camping only a few miles west of Gunshot.

"We'll hit the town at dawn," Colonel Blanchard announced. "I want a scout to go forward and reconnoiter."

"I need to go into Gunshot tonight," Longarm said. "I'll be the scout."

"That's out of the question. You could be caught and forced to reveal our presence."

"I could be . . . but I won't," Longarm vowed. "There are two good women that I have to deliver from Gunshot before we attack."

Colonel Blanchard looked pale and his voice had a tremor in it from the lack of alcohol, but was still in control. "Marshal, what you are proposing really is an unacceptable risk."

"I'm sorry," Longarm told the man. "But I have to get those women out in order to insure their safety. I can also learn if Trace Hall, their leader, is dead or alive. And, if he's alive, is he fit to take command? That's a very important thing to know."

"Why?"

"Because, if Trace is dead, the outlaws will be in turmoil and they might even surrender to your authority without their leader."

"All right," Blanchard agreed. "But I'll expect you to be back before daylight."

"I will be."

"I'm coming with you," Henry declared.

"It would be better if you stayed here with Colonel Blanchard and his soldiers."

"Please, Marshal Long, I know that I can help!"

Longarm relented. "All right. We'll ride as soon as it gets dark."

"I don't like this," Colonel Blanchard fretted. "But you're not under my command so I'll let this pass. However, if we hear gunshots from the outlaw's stronghold, we're going to attack immediately."

"That's your decision, but I'll promise you that Henry and I will be fine," Longarm assured the man as he checked his weapons and advised Henry to do the same.

They rode at sunset, and when they got close to Gunshot, they tethered their horses in the trees and sneaked into town on foot, then hid in a small shed behind the largest saloon, where Trace and the women lived in the upstairs level. Longarm could hear a lot of shouting and carousing, so he knew that the outlaws weren't expecting any trouble.

"Henry, you're going to have to follow me without a sound. If we run into someone, don't panic. Just keep your head down and your hat brim low. I'll do the talking."

"But—"

"Only shoot if I shoot first or am shot," Longarm added in a terse voice. "Is that clear?"

"Yes, sir."

"Come on, then."

He exited the shed and they walked without hurry over to the saloon, every muscle in their bodies stretched as tight as piano wire. When they stepped inside, Longarm kept in the shadows and moved along the wall listening to the loud voices and exceptional piano music. The outlaws were two deep at the bar and no one even noticed the two strangers.

"What do we do now?" Henry whispered.

"We listen and we learn," Longarm answered, leaning in toward Henry as if they were discussing something private.

During the next quarter hour, Longarm discovered that Trace was very much alive, but that he was convalescing upstairs. He also saw Rosa come down and mix among the outlaws a few minutes before heading back upstairs alone with a bottle of whiskey clenched in her hand.

"Henry, wait here. I'm going upstairs."

"I can't!"

"Why not?"

"What if someone asks me a question or tries to strike up a conversation?"

179

"Then just act unfriendly and mosey outside. If you hear shooting upstairs, duck in between the buildings and get to your horse. The most important thing is to tell Colonel Blanchard that Trace is alive and that he should go ahead and hit this town at sunrise with his soldiers shooting every man on sight."

"But what about *you*?"

"I'll be along. And, if I'm not, go ahead with the plan."

Henry started to protest, but Longarm grabbed him by the arm and squeezed hard. "You promised you'd follow my orders. Don't break your word to me!"

"No, sir."

Longarm left the young man. Averting his face from the crowded bar, he strolled across the saloon, mounted the stairs, and went up to Rosa's room without being challenged. When he knocked on her door, she replied. "Go away!"

Longarm turned the doorknob, but she'd thrown the dead bolt. "Rosa," he whispered, "it's Custis. Open up!"

A moment later the door flew open and Rosa was in his arms kissing his face and squealing with delight. He tried to close the door behind them, but she was kissing him so passionately that Longarm couldn't break free.

"Well, well," a sinister and contemptuous voice called a moment later. "If it isn't Custis Long returned to the arms of his passionate ladylove. How romantic! How incredibly stupid."

Longarm's hand stabbed for the gun on his hip, but Rosa's dress was in the way and he couldn't get free quick enough. He then tried to throw the woman aside and out of harm's way.

He was too late. Trace's bullet caught her in the back and Rosa screamed, then clutched him even harder as two more bullets tore into her body. By then, Longarm had found his Colt. His gun bucked in unison with Trace's fourth shot. Rosa's body stopped Trace's final bullet while Longarm's struck the leader in the mouth. The heavy slug tore through the outlaw's teeth, then exploded through his brain, spraying it and fragments of bone across the hallway to plaster the opposite wall.

"Rosa!"

She was dead.

Noleta appeared, and when she saw Longarm bending over Rosa's riddled body, she cried out in despair. The piano downstairs fell silent. In its place, Longarm heard angry and confused shouts.

"We've got to get out of here!" he urged, grabbing Noleta by the arm. He dragged her over Trace's body and they sprinted down the hallway looking for an escape.

"There's no way down!" Noleta cried. "And what about Rosa!"

"She's dead." Longarm could hear the pounding of feet on the stairway and knew they had only seconds left to hide. "Quick! Where's your room!"

"In here."

He opened the door and jerked her inside. He slammed the door and shot the bolt. Glancing around, Longarm spied the window and knew that it overlooked the main street. But there was no other way out of this death trap so he ran over, raised the window, and said, "Do you have anything to help lower us to the ground?"

"No!"

"Think hard, Noleta. There must be something we can tie together. How about your sheets?"

"There's no time for that," she said, hearing men already outside her door shouting that Trace had been shot.

Longarm stuck one of his legs out the second story window. "As soon as I jump, close the window and get in bed. Then pull the covers up to your neck, and when they bust down your door, tell them that you have a fever caused by smallpox or something infectious!"

Longarm didn't hear her response. He eased out the window until he was hanging full length, then let go and fell. He landed hard and his right ankle twisted sharply

181

under his weight. Jumping up, he tried to run, but the ankle betrayed him and he toppled facedown in the street.

"Marshal Long!" Henry shouted racing to his side.

Longarm pushed himself up to all fours, then onto one leg. He threw an arm across Henry's thin shoulders and yelled, "Let's get off the street before—"

"There he is!" someone cried as guns barked in the night. "He's the one that shot Trace again!"

Longarm and Henry dove for cover behind a water trough. They tried to return fire, but they were so outgunned that they were forced to keep their heads down low while the water trough was being riddled like a sieve.

"Things aren't looking good," Henry yelled over the roar of gunfire. "What are we going to do now!"

"Try to stay alive and wait for the United States cavalry! They'll try to flank us. You watch that side and I'll take this one. Don't let anyone cross the street."

Henry opened fire. Longarm didn't know if he killed his man or not, and there wasn't time to find out. The Gunshot Gang no longer had a leader, but they were as mad as hornets and a thousand times more deadly.

Chapter 17

It wasn't long at all before Colonel Blanchard and his cavalrymen charged into Gunshot with pistols blazing. The outlaws were so surprised, they must have thought that the town was being invaded by the entire United States Army because they either surrendered or were gunned down in the first deadly volley.

Longarm shot three men trying to climb up onto the roof and Henry shot at least two who chose to open fire on the cavalry. Colonel Avery Blanchard was the only soldier that died in the charge. Riding in the lead with, of all things, his saber waving like a banner overhead, the veteran officer probably died the way he'd always wanted . . . leading his troops into victory.

"We'll take care of them," Sergeant Veek said, rounding up the outlaws and having them frisked for hidden weapons then put under strict military guard.

Longarm went up and retrieved the beautiful Noleta from her bed. "Is it over?" she asked.

"Yes."

"What's going to happen to Gunshot now?"

Longarm thought about that for a moment. "Grab what is valuable while I recover all of Trace's stolen money. Tell the ladies to all leave with whatever they have to take of value. After that, I think Sergeant Veek will agree with me that Gunshot ought to be torched."

"Yes, that would be best so that others like Trace never come here."

So they gathered the gold, the money, and the stolen jewelry, and even a few sculptures and quality pieces of purloined artwork, and hauled it outside. Noleta took a few hundred dollars for herself as did the other women; the rest was left for Longarm to see that it was returned to its original owners.

The dead were collected and quickly buried. Rosa was the only one who merited a quick prayer and tears from her lady friends.

"Fire the town!" Sergeant Veek ordered, marching up and down the dark, now mostly empty, street.

The soldiers hurled torches into every building and then retreated to the edge of town to watch the inferno.

"Good-bye, Gunshot," Noleta said, unable to hide her bitterness.

Longarm took her arm and said, "I want you to meet my friend, Henry Evans. Without him, I might not have survived."

Henry became so flustered and shy he couldn't speak when he suddenly found himself standing before beautiful Noleta. Sensing his discomfort, she kissed his cheek and said, "Henry, you're an honest to goodness hero."

"Aw, shucks, miss!"

In the light of the inferno that ravaged Gunshot, Longarm could have sworn he could see Henry's cheeks burn.

It was a week before Longarm, Noleta, and Henry rode back to Lee's Ferry and stopped at Cozy Dell. Everything had changed, but most especially, Julie who didn't rush out to hug and kiss Longarm, but instead led handsome young Gavin out arm in arm.

"Good to see that you're on your feet, Gavin," Longarm

184

told the former outlaw. "Are you ready to go back to Cripple Creek and face a judge?"

"I am."

"I'm going with him," Julie declared. "Gavin needs my help, too."

Longarm didn't have to have eyes to see that Julie had fallen head over heels in love.

"All right," he said, looking at Caleb, his wife, and the other two women. "Then I guess we can all get on with our lives."

"Mind if I come along with you to Cripple Creek?" Noleta asked. "I hear that it's a wild and woolly town."

Longarm felt her slip her own arm through his own. "It is wild and woolly," he agreed, "but you might even like Denver better."

"That's where you live, isn't it?"

"Once in a while."

"Then I would like to go there with you."

Longarm glanced over at Julie and winked. She winked back and damned if everything didn't look as if it were going to turn out just fine . . . except for Billy Vail, who was surely going to lose his best and prettiest young office worker.

"Noleta, have you ever thought of working in an office?" Longarm asked.

"No."

"Maybe you should," he suggested. "I think I can get you a job."

"But, Custis, I don't know *anything* about offices."

"It doesn't matter," Julie said. "Believe me, you'll be hired."

"Well," Noleta replied. "I'll try anything . . . once."

Longarm thought that sounded just fine not only for Billy, but for himself. Furthermore, he could hardly wait to get this beautiful woman all alone in a gently rocking train compartment.

Watch for

**LONGARM AND THE DENVER
EXECUTIONERS**

275th novel in the exciting LONGARM series
from Jove

Coming in October!

Explore the exciting Old West with one of the men who made it wild!